UNASSISTED LIVING

Bob Puglisi

bpbooks2014@yahoo.com

Cover design by Kym O'Connell-Todd

Bob Puglisi's photograph by Robert DeLaurenti

ISBN:978-1987490725

For all my friends and relatives of a certain age.

Also by Bob Puglisi

Novels
Railway Avenue
Midnight Auto Supply

Memoir
Almost A Wiseguy

CHAPTER 1
1975

The sun's first rays broke the early morning darkness, and a shimmer of daylight silhouetted the Manhattan skyline. A Staten Island Ferry floated into its berth and docked. A steady stream of commuters rushed off the boat. Some people headed towards lower Manhattan office buildings and Wall Street, others descended into the subway and some stepped onto city transit buses. A New York Daily News truck unloaded bundles of newspapers at one of the newspaper stands in front of the ferry terminal. The bold-faced headline on the front page read: SENIORS BATTLE CITY. Commuters coming off the ferry stopped to pick up their copies.

In another part of the city, the Westside Produce Market was abuzz with activity. Men pushed hand trucks with crates and cardboard boxes filled with produce from loading docks onto waiting trucks. Trucks and vans pulled in and out of the market. Traffic in the area was mostly at a standstill with honking horns and men shouting and cursing at one another as they attempted to get in and out of the market area.

A sign over one of the loading docks displayed the name: SAMBUCCI'S PRODUCE. Several workers loaded a waiting truck with boxes of produce. From the looks of some of the product, it didn't look edible.

Mildred Meyers, a petite, white-haired seventy-year-old came out of the building onto the dock trailed by Angelo Sambucci, a large, overweight and balding man in his sixties. Mildred shouted at the men pushing hand trucks onto the waiting truck, "Stack them tight." The men nodded politely in her direction.

Mildred and Angelo had a long friendship. Until she retired a few years earlier, Mildred was the bookkeeper for Sambucci Produce. That entailed also running the office, answering the telephone, taking orders over the phone, helping with inventories and cleaning. She helped Angelo through good and bad times. Now, occasionally, she came to see how the new bookkeeper was doing and to chat with Angelo. This morning she was there for another purpose.

Angelo was very grateful to Mildred for her loyalty through the years and her hard work. This was payback day for Angelo. He stood next to her, squinted his right eye, and said, "But you're crazy."

Mildred ignored him and glanced at her digital watch with its large easy-to-read numbers. With steam coming from her mouth on that frigid morning, she looked out at the bottlenecked traffic, then at the men loading the truck, and said, "Come on. Hurry up! We'll never get out of here with all this traffic." Then to Angelo she said, "I hope that's the rottenness stuff you have."

He raised a hand with his palm out, and said, "What? I'm gonna give ya the fresh stuff?"

With a smile on her face, Mildred laughed. Angelo leveled his gaze at her and took a serious tone, "Why don't ya just move? I got a nice building in Bensonhurst with an empty apartment. I'll take ya to see it."

"I can find an apartment. It's the principle."

"Ah, you and principle," he waved a hand at her.

Mildred looked at her watch again. "If I move anywhere, it's gonna be Hawaii!"

"Hawaii? You're nuts. What the hell ya gonna do there?"

"They got warm weather."

"What's wrong with New York weather?"

She looked at him. "Ang, I can't take this cold anymore." She pulled her coat collar snug around her neck.

"Ya know ya can't win with that Daniels guy. He owns half the city."

"Yeah, well he's just a fat little blowhard."

"You're gonna get yourself in a lot of trouble. I don't want to read about you again in the papers tomorrow."

Mildred had been an activist all her adult life, maybe even as a child. Just name an issue or an injustice and Mildred probably protested it—a roadway through Washington Square Park, the bomb, the Vietnam War, women's rights, South African apartheid, civil rights in which she marched alongside Dr. Martin Luther King Jr. She was friends with Eleanor Roosevelt, who stood with Mildred at several protests. Mildred acquired, at an early age, her mother, Rosie Rabinovitz's, energy and spunk. When Mildred's mother suffered a severe bout of pneumonia, twelve-year-old Mildred cared for her mom and did all the cooking, cleaning, and caring for her brothers and sisters.

The last hand truck emptied its load and exited the truck. Mildred looked around. "Who's driving?"

Angelo said, "I'm gonna drive ya. I wanna get my truck back in one piece." Mildred climbed into the passenger seat.

A little while later, the produce truck made its way slowly through the morning congestion of the Lower East Side. Angelo kept his eyes on the traffic ahead. Mildred glanced at her watch; Angelo looked at his and said, "Don't worry, we'll be there soon."

As they reached Mildred's street and turned the corner, a barricade of sandbags, furniture and junk stopped them about halfway down the street. Behind it, elderly men and women stood guard. They dressed in WWII helmets, army surplus fatigues, football helmets and shoulder pads. The south side of the street looked like London following the blitz with just two tenements standing, an empty lot between the buildings indicating a similar building had once stood there. Nothing but rubble surrounded them. On both sides of the remaining structures, idle bulldozers sat silently, aimed maliciously at the old tenements. There was also a fifty-foot-high crane with a steel wrecking ball sitting on the ground just a few feet from the building nearest the blockade. A large white sign, supported by two posts, said, DANIELS DEVELOPMENT NO TRESPASSING. Twenty or thirty yards down the street, there was another barricade to the right of the furthest tenement. The tenements across the street stood untouched, but for how long, their residents wondered.

Between the barricades, fifty or sixty people of all ages milled about preparing for battle. Mildred stuck her head out the truck window. “Get that thing open so we can get through!” she shouted to the elderly men behind it. They hopped to it, making an opening just wide enough for the truck to pass. With her head out the window, the truck drove through and Mildred ordered, “And don’t let anyone else in!”

An old man shouted up to Mildred, “They said the cops are on their way.”

“We’ll be ready for them,” Mildred called back.

The truck pulled in front of the first tenement. Mildred and Angelo got out. With his hands on his hips, Angelo looked at the buildings with disdain.

“All right—everyone help us unload,” Mildred directed.

The tailgate dropped and a few younger men wearing camouflage fatigues jumped into the truck and started pushing boxes to the rear. Mildred noticed Angelo staring at her soon-to-be demolished tenement, an old, red brick building with an abandoned storefront that had three stories and a fire escape above the street level. She came alongside. He turned to her and said, “This is what you’re fighting for. Without that building between them, they’re gonna fall down.”

Mildred knew he was right, but she was not giving up her home of over thirty years without a fight. “I told you it’s the principle.”

Angelo waved a dismissive hand at her. They looked back to the truck; old and young people loaded boxes on wagons and supermarket shopping carts and pushed them towards the barricades. “Put some in-between, too!” Mildred instructed at the top of her voice.

After they whisked away the last box, Angelo said, "Awright, I'm getting' the hell out of here. You should too."

Mildred gave him a you-got-to-be-kidding look. Angelo said, "Yeah, that's what I figured. It's the principle!" He laughed and then hugged her. "You be careful. You're not young anymore."

"I'll be fine."

"Yeah, yeah…"

Mildred turned to a twentyish Puerto Rican man and said, "Open up so he can get out. And make sure it's closed tight once he gets through."

"Gotcha Mildred."

Angelo got into the truck and waited for a passage to open in front of him, and then he pulled the truck down the street and turned the corner.

CHAPTER 2

At the Manhattan South Police Headquarters, police dressed in riot gear filed into waiting buses. Four men in business suits got into a car with NEW YORK CITY MARSHAL inscribed on the side. The marshal's car, police cruisers and vans pulled away in a long line.

Shortly after, police and city marshals stepped out of their vehicles and assembled into a formation facing one of Mildred's walls.

A long black limo made its way past the buses and cars and stopped. The driver opened the back door. Calvin Daniels, the fifty-eight year-old New York real estate tycoon responsible for the conflict, stepped out. He was short and squat, slightly balding with a bad comb-over, and had beady eyes. He walked up to the wall. The elderly gentlemen standing guard stuck their middle fingers in the air. Daniels scowled at them, turned away and walked over to a tall, beefy police captain carrying a bullhorn. "I want these people out of here today. This nonsense is costing me money," he said.

"Don't worry. We'll take care of it Mr. Daniels."

Daniels' condominium developments were always contentious, and based on past experience, Daniels knew he would prevail in the end.

CHAPTER 3

Mildred stood on an empty wooden crate in front of her tenement; her supporters and sympathizers assembled before her. They were a ragtag group of elderly and younger people. Mildred said, "Now's the time to fight—not tomorrow when our homes are rubble. For those of you my age you know how important a home is. We're tired of being bullied into doing things we don't want just because we're old." The crowd roared with enthusiasm. "We must be able to do what we want with our lives and not have others decide our fate." They cheered again. "And you younger people—what happens here today will affect your lives, too."

Meanwhile, outside the barricades, more police arrived in riot gear. Some of them listened to the rallying cries coming from inside Mildred's defenses. A bevy of news media, CBS, NBC and ABC prepared to report on the confrontation about to take place.

"Now let's get out there and fight for our rights! Man your positions! You ladies, too!" Mildred said forcefully as she proudly reviewed her troops. A powerful feeling came over her, making her hopeful for a successful conclusion. Another boisterous cheer rose from the crowd as they took up positions at the walls and prepared to throw their fruits and vegetables.

Beyond the barricade, a police captain stood on the roof of a police car with a bullhorn to his mouth. "Can I have your attention please?"

The protestors responded, "Pigs go home! Leave us alone!" Someone yelled, "Attica! Attica!" Others joined in. An old guy shouted over the wall, "Daniels—eat shit!"

Daniels turned around quickly upon hearing his name. He scowled in the direction of the taunt.

The news folks surrounded the captain and pointed microphones and cameras in his direction.

With the determination of a military commander, Mildred made her way to the barricade facing the cops. One of the men helped Mildred onto a stepladder so she could see the enemy. She listened as the police captain continued, "This is your final chance to give up this fight and let the demolition work continue."

He had to stop speaking because of the roar from the group between the walls, and the people gathered on the sidewalks and street behind him. They included folks from surrounding streets who feared the demise of their own homes. When it quieted enough for him, he continued, "The city marshal's office has given us the authority to peacefully evict you." There were more jeers. "You have five minutes to open up and step aside!" The crowd responded with boos and catcalls. Several people started throwing produce at the captain. He ducked a few missiles and didn't look happy about it. Before getting down from his pulpit, he said, "We don't want to have to arrest anyone."

A disbelieving look crossed Mildred's face.

"Mrs. Meyers! Mrs. Meyers!" a news reporter shouted, "How will you respond to these threats?"

She smiled back and said, "We're prepared to fight." Her supporters cheered her on.

Someone in the crowd shouted, "Seniors have rights!" Others chimed in and they all chanted, "Seniors have rights! Seniors have rights!"

A female newsperson with a cameraman beside her asked, "Are these rundown buildings worth being arrested, even injured?"

Mildred responded, "Many of us raised families here. These buildings have sentimental value. They have been our homes for over thirty years. To cast us out on the street is a black mark on the City of New York. They've been tearing this neighborhood apart piece by piece for decades. It has to stop here and now."

She climbed down from the ladder with the media hurling more questions at her. "What will happen next? How many years have you lived here? Do you consider Calvin Daniels your enemy?" Mildred's supporters cheered with enthusiasm and patted her on the back.

Mildred walked over to an older bent woman, her friend and neighbor for over thirty years, Hattie Ryan. Hattie opened her arms and the two women hugged. "I'm scared Mildred."

"I know," Mildred said. "You shouldn't be out here. You should watch from the window."

"I wanna sock that Daniels."

"If I get a chance, I'll sock him for you. How do you feel?"

With a huge smile, she said, "Like fighting!" She made a fist with her little gloved hand and punched it into the air in a power salute. Taking her hand down, she said, "Ooo that hurt," and rubbed her shoulder.

"You better take it easy, tiger." Mildred smiled and buttoned Hattie's coat. "Stay warm or you'll get sick. Why don't you go upstairs and watch?"

Hattie puffed out her chest. She smiled at Mildred as she took a large can of Ready Whip out of her coat pocket. "I'll get them good before they get me."

A woman shouted, "Mildred come on! We're running out of time."

Mildred turned back to Hattie. "Now you be careful."

"You be careful, too!" Hattie hugged Mildred.

"You have one minute! One minute left!" came through the bullhorn.

Mildred's troops responded with more jeers. She and Hattie separated; Mildred pushed her way through the crowd and yelled, "Get ready to fight!"

Everyone roared with excitement and got closer to the barricades as they pulled wagons and shopping carts piled high with rotten goods. Mildred looked at the boxes of rotten stuff stacked in front of the walls in easy reach for throwing. She made her way to the front of her rebel band. The captain's voice crackled again through the bullhorn, "Your time is up. Now, please stand down." The police started to move forward. They dressed in full riot gear with clear plastic Kevlar shields raised in front of them.

Mildred responded by addressing her troops, "Get ready!"

The police continued to march forward.

Mildred waited until the police were only steps away and yelled, "Ready… Fire!"

A barrage of fruit and vegetables flew over the wall and splattered the police despite their shields. As they got closer and tried to dismantle the barricade, they were surprised by streams of whipped cream and shaving cream flying through the air. Someone helped Hattie up on a box so she could get in her licks. She laughed hysterically as her whipped cream sailed over the shields and hit the police. They retreated in an attempt to regroup. Flying eggs splattered them. Safely out of range, Calvin Daniels arrogantly watched with a smirk on his face. The encounter left the police stunned, confused, disorganized, and covered in crud.

Calvin Daniels, a man used to getting his way, turned to the captain and said, "This is the New York City Police Department running away from a disgusting bunch of little, frail, old farts…"

The captain had a sympathetic look on his face, and spoke in a reassuring voice, "Mister Daniels, we're doing our job the best we can. Because of the age of these people, we are approaching the situation with sensitivity. We don't want to make the city look any worse than we already do." The captain looked like he wanted to say more but knew his place.

"Just get those people off my property. I want them out of here today. Time is money. I'll be calling Mayor Beame later if this isn't resolved today—and there will be a price to pay."

The captain didn't like the inference and tried to ignore it. "Don't worry. We'll take care of it Mr. Daniels."

Mildred and her people celebrated a brief victory. She scurried among them, preparing them for the next assault, while on the other side of the barricade, the police milled around trying to clean themselves off. In a few minutes, they re-grouped into another formation about to charge the barricade. Another group of about twenty or thirty cops moved off away from the action. More police joined those about to make another thrust forward.

As soon as the police were in range again, Mildred and her cohorts threw everything they had at them. This time the police held their shields over their heads and made it all the way to the barricade. Despite the heavy bombardment, they started to pull Mildred's defenses apart. Mildred and her warriors kept up an endless barrage from their arsenal. One old woman swung a broom at the advancing police. Unbeknownst to Mildred and her gang, some of the cops that had marched away were now coming up the street behind Mildred's rear.

Before Mildred and her troops could react, the cops were breaking through that barricade. Mildred's folks threw their cache of artillery in both directions. Mildred, annoyed with herself for not doing a better job of protecting her rear, was about to shout something to her people when a police officer grabbed her from behind. She managed to wriggle free and dodge the officer's attempt to reel her in again. At that point, it all seemed futile to her. The police tore apart the barricades and rushed through the gaping holes. Mildred ran to help some elderly people who were fighting off the police by swinging umbrellas like swords, others attempted judo and karate, and rotten produce flew in all directions. The protest was all but over. The police grabbed more and more people, arrested them and whisked them away.

Mildred and those around her continued fighting back, but she knew things were not going in their favor.

They were badly outnumbered. A police officer twice her size attempted to grab her. She kicked him in the shins, but he managed to get hold of her coat, push her to the ground then handcuff her behind the back. With her face pressed against the cold asphalt, a feeling of crushing disappointment came over her and she felt like crying. The cop pulled her to her feet and then led her away, half pulling her as she continued to resist. Mildred staggered along, watching her youthful followers absorb the violence the police were hesitant to inflict on the elderly folks. Mildred kicked and wriggled as the policeman dragged her to a waiting van. "I have my rights! Let me go! I have my rights!"

They pushed Mildred into the van and threw more people in behind her. Those already inside booed when they saw the rough treatment Mildred received.

CHAPTER 4

Mildred's thirty-three-year-old daughter, Nancy Meyers, lived in a modern-looking house on a Hollywood hillside with her boyfriend, Jeff Kress, a forty-year-old, handsome, graying, television producer. Jeff had several series on the air, mostly TV dramas. He had a charming personality and was used to the finer things.

Nancy, a prima ballerina, danced all over the world and attributed much of her success to her mother's support. She never knew her father who left them when she was born, taking all their savings and leaving them almost destitute. Mildred devoted her life to her daughter and worked in order to give her a good education. Nancy started dance classes at the age of four. By the time she was five, she had performed in recitals. Her teachers considered her a gifted child, both artistically and scholastically. Her mother enrolled her in a private elementary school where she could cultivate her dancing abilities.

Most of Nancy's schoolmates were from wealthy New York families who lived in affluent Manhattan neighborhoods, unlike Nancy who lived in a Lower East Side tenement. She loved her mom but sometimes felt her mother was not like friends' mothers, who didn't work and were stay-at-home moms. Nancy tried her best not to reveal that her mom was a bookkeeper at the produce market.

When Nancy was high school age, New York's High School of Performing Arts, a tuition-free public school, accepted her into their program. It provided some financial freedom for Mildred, but the extra money went to pay for private dance lessons with some of New York's finest ballet teachers. Mildred never complained about the expenses and often exchanged bookkeeping services for Nancy's lessons. After high school, Nancy went to Julliard. While there, a choreographer for the New York City Ballet Company hired her for his corps of dancers. After that, she moved up quickly through the company. Her first big break was Aurora in *Sleeping Beauty*, for which she received rave reviews. At nineteen, Nancy was touring the world with aspirations for more and more challenging roles.

When the phone rang that morning, the couple was still in bed. Jeff answered then handed the phone to a half-asleep Nancy. "Hello? This was not the first time her mother's lawyer surprised her with an early morning phone call from New York. "Yes, I'm fine. What is it? She what? Oh, no. I don't know. All right. I'll try to get a flight today. Bye." Nancy handed the phone back to Jeff.

"Who was that?"

"My mother's been arrested again for inciting a riot. And I don't know, a whole bunch of other charges. That was her lawyer. I have to go to New York to get her out of jail."

"When?"

"Today, if I can get a flight."

"Can't he get her out?

"He said they want me to be there to take custody of her."

"And what are you going to do with her?"

"I don't know yet. Maybe bring her here?"

"In our house?"

"Jeff, it's my mother. What else am I going to do with her?"

"Find her a place to live like I did for my mother. You want your mother living with us?"

"I don't know." Nancy got out of bed, picked up a white robe off the chair beside the bed and put it over her slim, curvaceous body with its white alabaster skin. Jeff sat up in bed. Gray hairs speckled his bare chest. "What about the dinner party at the Mayfield's tonight?"

"You'll have to go by yourself."

"You know how important this is to our project."

"Jeff! What am I supposed to do. It's my mother. What am I going to leave her in jail?"

Jeff grimaced and got out of bed. Standing naked he watched her go into the bathroom.

The Mayfield's were key investors in a TV project for PBS in which Nancy would dance the role of Giselle in the ballet of the same name. It would be the fulfillment of a lifetime career dream.

A white Porsche 924 pulled into the oval driveway of Jeff's house. Karen Eichel, about the same age as Nancy, was an attractive blonde; the two women could almost pass for sisters. They met at Julliard. Over the years, they competed for many of the same roles, but Karen always knew Nancy had a natural talent that Karen lacked. They worked hard at their craft and shared their deepest secrets. Karen opened the car door and stretched her long legs encased in black tights to the ground. With her hair in a ponytail, wearing a large white pullover sweater and black high-top sneakers, she made her way to the front door and rang the bell. Jeff opened the large wooden door. He smiled and said seductively, "Oh, hello Karen."

"Hi Jeff!" She smiled back as she brushed past him. Karen liked Jeff and wished her best friend would appreciate him more. In her mind, he was a great catch.

"She's in the kitchen."

An overnight black suitcase sat inside the door. Karen made her way into the modern kitchen with an expansive view of the city. She sensed something askew as she admired how attractive Nancy looked in a black pantsuit. Her shoulder-length hair hung around her face as she sipped coffee from a mug and munched on a bagel with cream cheese. As Karen got closer, she looked more concerned and asked, "Hey, you all right?"

"I'm feeling a little tired. It's probably my age. I know I can't keep dancing forever.

"Any news on those choreographer jobs?"

"No, nothing yet." Nancy glanced across the room for Jeff, realizing he was already in another part of the house. "Did you see Jeff?"

"Yes."

"He's being a real asshole today."

Karen seemed to understand the situation. She knew about the couple's troubled relationship. Nancy and Jeff had been together three years. They both fooled around with other people but still managed to stay together out of convenience, or for some reason that Karen couldn't figure out; maybe it was love.

Nancy toured often with her dance troupe and Jeff traveled extensively, making it difficult to be monogamous for either of them.

"You want some coffee?"

"Sure." Karen moved closer to the counter as Nancy removed a cup from a cabinet, filled it, and placed it in front of her friend. "Did you have an argument?"

Nancy lowered her voice, "Yes. I have to get a place of my own. I wanted to bring my mother here. He won't let me. He says, he refused to take his mother in—why would he want mine here?"

Karen smiled, "That's pretty insensitive."

"Yes. That's the problem."

"She'd probably be cleaning this place from morning to night. You know how your mother is."

"Will she come to LA?"

"I don't know—she's so independent. She's been talking about Hawaii the last few years. She loves it there."

"Wouldn't that be good for her?"

Nancy screwed up her face. "I don't know. It's just as far away from here as New York. I can still get to New York faster if she needs me. There's more flights."

"I don't know about that."

"She doesn't approve of my living with Jeff, anyway. She wants me to get married again." Karen looked at Nancy like she had heard this many times. They both sipped their coffee in silence.

Nancy had married a West Point cadet who she met at an elaborate party given by the director of her ballet company. The couple had a beautiful ceremony in which they walked under swords held over their heads by his fellow cadets. Immediately after graduation, Gerald Fowler, then twenty-two, received orders for Vietnam. Three months into his tour, the Viet Cong ambushed his company and the young lieutenant perished. It devastated Nancy so much that she took a year off from dance to recover her sanity.

"Maybe I can find her a place to live here in LA? Maybe a two bedroom we can share when I'm in town."

"You want to live with your mother?"

"Not really."

"How about my friend Stanley's retirement home?"

"Oh, she would never stand for any old-age home."

"It's not like that. It's a private house with only a few people. They're a bunch of independent old people, a lot like your mother."

Nancy thought a little more seriously that it might be a good place for her mom.

"Stanley… is that the cute guy you met the day your car broke down."

"Yes. He tried to get it to start, then he waited with me until the tow truck came and drove me home. We've had a couple of dates. He's a sweet guy."

"That's nice."

"Maybe we can stop and see him on our way to the airport. It's right here in Hollywood. I'll call him." She went over to the phone and picked it up.

CHAPTER 5

Karen's Porsche pulled up in front of the Star Bright Senior Residence. The women got out. Nancy looked reluctantly at the two-story craftsman house on this quiet residential street in Hollywood. The outside was in desperate need of repairs and a paint job. Similar houses on the street were in better shape. Across the street and down the same side as Star Bright were several apartment buildings from three to six stories. They walked through the front yard and smelled the fragrance of recently cut grass. Nancy said, "It looks a little rundown."

"Yeah, it is but it's cute inside."

Stanley Cutler met them at the door. He was a spacey looking hippy in his early thirties who wore extremely thick glasses that made his eyes look like tiny dots, and he had dark brown, long shoulder-length hair. He looked up at Nancy and Karen who were both several inches taller than him. He and Karen hugged. "I was surprised when you called. I thought you were still out of town."

"I got back on Sunday. Stanley, this is Nancy."

"Nice to meet you."

They entered the house and he led them into his crammed little office just to the right of the entrance. Stanley sat down behind an old wooden desk.

"Have a seat," he said, pointing to a worn wooden church bench against the wall opposite his desk. "There's a UCLA basketball game tomorrow night. Are you free?"

"I'd love to go," Karen said.

"I can pick you up around six."

"Why don't I pick you up at six?"

"Okay. We can get something to eat in Westwood before the game.

"It sounds like fun."

"Can I get you anything?" Stanley asked.

"We don't have a lot of time. Nancy has to get to the airport."

Nancy stared at the display cases with toy soldiers that hung from the walls behind the desk. A number of intricate model ships and airplanes sat on top of bookcases and cabinets around the room. She looked to the left, through a doorway, into another smaller room with an unmade bed. Stanley's unkempt bedroom and his messy office wasn't giving her a favorable impression.

Nancy asked, "How long have you had this place?"

"It was my mother's. She had cancer. I came here—I guess about four years ago from San Francisco, when they diagnosed her. She passed away two years ago."

"I'm sorry to hear that," Nancy said.

"Everybody helped me get through it. The folks who live here are wonderful. Wait till you meet them. I don't know what I would have done without them." He opened a desk drawer and took out two packages of Twinkies. "Would you like some?"

The women both shook their heads, refusing. "How many people live here?" Nancy asked.

Stanley seemed to be counting as he opened one of the packages and took a Twinkie out.

"Five." Then, he bit into the Twinkie.

"Do you have room for one more?

"As I told Karen on the phone, the timing is perfect. Mrs. Palmer just moved out to live with her son in Wisconsin. So I have an empty room."

Hesitantly, Nancy answered, "Oh… that's good. Do you have activities?"

He picked up a bottle of Coke and sipped before answering. "Activities? I'm sorry we don't. Everyone is on their own. They like it that way. I call it unassisted living." He smiled at his cleverness. The girls didn't react. "Mrs. Bennetti likes to go to the race track." Nancy raised an eyebrow, and then looked doubtfully at Karen. "Mr. and Mrs. Benson like to go for walks and other things," he said with a mischievous expression on his face. Nancy and Karen looked at each other but didn't say anything. "Everyone always seems to have something to do. To be honest, if that's the kind of place you're looking for, there are plenty of them around. I try to keep this as close to a real home as possible. People just come and go as they please. Besides, I can't afford activities. I don't make much money. If I can ever figure out these books…" He pointed to a couple of large black ledgers on the desk. He continued, "I'm afraid I'll find out how much money I'm losing." Nancy gazed around the room, somewhat uncertain.

"My mother's an extremely active woman."

"That's good. Then, she might like it here."

"Hmm…" Nancy sighed.

"Why don't you show Nancy the rest of the house, Stanley?"

He jumped out of his seat. "Oh, sure."

The women followed him out of the room."

CHAPTER 6

The demonstration made the New York evening news. That night a TV news anchor said, "A riot broke out this morning on New York City's Lower East Side when a makeshift band of mostly senior citizens fought the police and city marshals trying to evict them from their homes in order to make way for a new condominium development. The rioters bombarded authorities with rotten fruit, vegetables, and the contents of spray cans. As a result, the group's leader, Mildred Meyers, a seventy-year old, was taken into custody and charged with several counts. When we interviewed her prior to the riot, Meyers said, 'We're tired of being bullied into doing things we don't want just because we're old.' We also spoke to Calvin Daniels, the New York real estate developer behind the project, and he said, 'These tenements are the worst of the city's urban decay. Once these buildings are gone, they will be replaced by modern streamlined condominiums that will improve the quality of life of the entire Lower East Side. This is only the first step in a complete redevelopment of the community.'"

Calvin Daniels' family had been the face of New York real estate development for more than a century. They were responsible for the construction of many of

Manhattan's early skyscrapers. John Daniels, Calvin's father, was a ruthless executive who cared less about the little guy and more about his growing fortunes. He displaced thousands of people in order to achieve his goals. Upon graduation from college, Calvin joined his father's firm and continued his father's legacy with little respect for anyone in his way. Daniels hands were all over most of the condo development in New York, California, Florida, and Hawaii. His vision for New York City's future was to re-gentrify the entire Lower East Side, leveling entire blocks of rundown tenements, and displacing its residents, mostly the elderly, poor whites, Hispanics, and blacks by using whatever methods, good or bad, at his disposal to oust residents. Court dockets were filled with numerous lawsuits against him and his company over his corrupt business practices and unconscionable eviction of tenants from their homes.

CHAPTER 7

Mildred's arrest landed her in New York City's Women's House of Detention, a depressingly old, red brick building. It had a reputation for being a hellhole. From the building, a gaggle of women's voices bellowed out to the street below. Police and visitors entered and left through a large steel door at the front of the building.

Mildred shared a cell with two women. Most of Mildred's accomplices posted bail and went home. She alone remained detained, waiting for Nancy's arrival. Mildred paced nervously within the small cell. A white prostitute in her thirties, wearing too much makeup and a dirty blond wig, stretched out on one of the lower bunks. Above her, a large black woman in her forties with dreadlocks sat propped against the wall in a lotus position. It was obvious she had been here before. She indignantly watched Mildred pacing.

Mildred said, "I wish I had my knitting."

"They wouldn't let ya have knitting needles," the black woman answered sarcastically.

"I know." Mildred stopped pacing when a female guard appeared with a frightened teenage girl. The guard opened the cell door, nudged the girl inside, and then locked the door with a distinct metallic clang. The girl threw herself face down on Mildred's bed, releasing a loud sob. The black woman said, "Oh, Christ!" She and the blonde woman looked at the teenager with disdain. The girl was not about to get any sympathy from them.

Mildred asked the guard, "What's she doing here?"

"Ask her!" The guard said, then turned and walked away.

Mildred turned around, looked at the girl, and said, "That's my bed."

The girl sprung upright. A worried look came over her. "It's alright," Mildred offered. She looked at the other two and said to the girl, "Just ignore them."

For a brief moment, it looked as though that put her at ease, until she shook uncontrollably and released another long sob. It got the attention of some of the women in the adjoining cells. Someone shouted, "Whatta they puttin' a kid like that in here for?" It unleashed a cacophony of remarks from other inmates. "Get her the fuck outta here!" "She's just a baby." "Pigs! Pigs!"

As the outcry subsided, Mildred sat down next to the girl. Mildred figured she was a good kid who made a big mistake. Unlike many of the inmates, she was clean cut and wore too-tight Jordache jeans, and her dirty blond hair looked expensively cut. She was pretty and through her tears large brown eyes glanced nervously at her surroundings.

Mildred placed a calming hand over the girl's clasped hands and said softly, "What are you doing here?"

The girl wiped tears from her cheeks on the shirtsleeve of her starched white blouse. "I was arrested for shoplifting."

"It must be a mistake," Mildred said.

The girl shook again but seemed all cried out. "We thought it was gonna be fun. We..." she took a deep breath, "...never thought this was gonna happen."

"Who's we?"

"My boyfriend and me."

She started to cry again. Mildred looked at the other two women and said, "Get her some water." The prostitute got off her bunk slowly, stepped over to the sink, and filled a paper cup. She handed it to Mildred and lay back down on her bed. Mildred held the cup up to the girl's lips. "Here drink some water." The girl gulped the water greedily. "Take it easy... Everything is going to be okay." Mildred's words and the water seemed to calm the young woman. "Where's your boyfriend, now?"

"I don't... know..." She half-cried the words. "They... separated us... at the police station."

"Have you ever done this before?"

"No never. It was his idea."

"What did you steal?"

"Nothing. Well, we were trying to steal perfume and cologne at Bloomingdales. They caught us going out the door with them."

"Huh! Listen to this one—Bloomingdales! That is stealin', honey," the black woman said with an arrogant smirk on her face.

Mildred threw her a you're-not-helping look. The woman shrugged her shoulders. "They'll go easy on you. Your poor parents. Do you have parents?"

"Yes."

"Do they know?"

"They let me call them from the police station.

They said they'd come and get me out."

Mildred seemed at a loss for words. She looked around at her surroundings, thinking about what she was doing there as well. "Look at this place. Is this the kind of life you want?"

The girl looked up as though noticing the reality of her surroundings for the first time. "What's an old lady like you doing here?" she asked.

Mildred stared hopelessly at the girl, wondering the same thing.

CHAPTER 8

By the time Nancy and Mr. Lewis, Mildred's attorney, arrived at the detention center, it was late evening. He was a short man, probably about the same age as Mildred. He had an unkempt appearance, wore a wrinkled black suit, glasses, and a brown fedora and carried a leather attaché case. He walked slowly, causing Nancy to adjust her long-legged stride to his pace. Mr. Lewis said, "I would have had her out on bail… You wouldn't have had to come all this way. But your mother gave the judge a hard time." He emphasized "hard time." "She doesn't understand that he doesn't care about the plight of senior citizens in this city." The attorney opened the front door for Nancy and they entered the lobby of the building. Mr. Lewis removed paperwork from his briefcase and handed it to the officer behind the window. "This is Mrs. Meyers' daughter. We'd like to see her."

The officer said, "I'll get someone to take you in, Mr. Lewis. If you can just wait over there," pointing to a long bench to the left.

"Thank you."

After a few minutes, an electronic door opened and another officer signaled them to follow him. They walked down a long hallway to another locked door. The officer opened it with a key. They entered a private room with glass windows all around it, a table and several chairs. “They’re bringing her down. Have a seat!” the officer said. He left and Nancy and Mr. Lewis sat at the table.

After a few minutes, the door on the other side of the room opened and Mildred entered. Nancy jumped up. Mildred hurried to her daughter and they hugged. Nancy asked, “Ma, are you all right?”

“Me…? I’m fine.”

“What’s that scrape on your face?”

“Oh, that. They roughed me up a little before I got arrested.”

“Police brutality that’s what it is,” Mr. Lewis, mentioned indignantly. Nancy looked upset by what she was hearing and touched the wound. Mildred flinched a little.

The women separated and Mildred held her daughter at arm’s length; she looked Nancy up and down. “You look tired and lost weight. I hope you are eating all right.”

“Ma, I’ve been eating. No problems.” In the past, Nancy had eating disorders, somewhat common among her peers.

Mildred felt her daughter’s waist and said, “No meat… There’s no meat on you. How’s your knees?”

“Mom! Never mind that… We have to get you out of here.”

“You taking those vitamins I sent you?”

“Yes.”

“They’re very good. I take them myself.”

“Let’s sit down,” Nancy suggested, and they sat.

Mildred stared at Nancy's purse. "Where'd you get that purse? It looks expensive. How much did you pay for it? I saw one just like that at Klein's."

Nancy and Mr. Lewis exchanged frustrated glances. Mildred said, "I hope you are saving your money? You know you can't dance forever." She turned her attention to the attorney. "I just met a young girl in here who can use a good lawyer," Mildred said.

"Does she have a family?" Mr. Lewis asked.

"She said she does."

"I'm sure they have their own attorney. It's you we have to take care of."

"Mom, I found a nice place for you to live in L.A."

"But I don't like L.A. I told you when I leave New York I'm going to Hawaii." She touched Nancy's hair. "I like your hair cut like this." Nancy looked exasperated.

"Mildred, the only way you're getting out of here is to go with your daughter."

"What if I don't want to?"

"I'm afraid you have no choice. The judge is being lenient with you so please be cooperative."

"Ma, it's the only option you have."

"Oh, that's nonsense."

"I'm afraid not, Mildred. We have a court appearance in the morning. If you agree to the judge's terms and go to L.A. with Nancy, they'll release you right away."

Mildred became uncharacteristically quiet. "Ma, please do this for me."

"I'll think about it. That's all I'm gonna say for now."

"Alright, we're going to go now. We'll see you in the morning."

CHAPTER 9

The next morning, Mr. Lewis, Nancy and Mildred stood in front of Judge Coates, a black man in his fifties. His old, wood paneled courtroom overflowed with people. The judge read from his docket, "Inciting a riot, disorderly conduct, criminal mischief, assaulting a police officer, resisting arrest… The charges go on for another half page." He looked up. "Ms. Meyers, your mother can receive an extremely stiff sentence. This isn't the first time she has been in my court. I can literally throw the book at her."

Nancy shifted nervously. Mildred had to resist saying anything as her lawyer had advised. The judge, staring down at Mildred, continued, "But this is the most disgraceful of all your escapades."

Mildred couldn't take it any longer and said, "Have you ever been evicted from your home?"

He looked sternly at her. "That's beside the point. I'm not on trial here."

Mildred looked up at him expecting an answer. "Have you?... Well?"

Judge Coates sat up straight in his chair and scowled at Mildred through piercing eyes, before answering. "Yes, I have. As a matter of fact, when I was a young boy in Newark, my family and I experienced an eviction from our apartment. And, we didn't go attacking the authorities."

His words seemed to go right over Mildred's head. "This city has pushed senior citizens around long enough and—"

"You're out of order Mrs. Meyers!"

Nancy grabbed her mother's arm and shook her. "Ma, quiet!" Nancy whispered.

"Will you please be quiet for your own good?" Mr. Lewis asked.

"Mr. Lewis and I have conferred with the district attorney. Has your attorney discussed this with you?"

Mildred had a stubborn look on her face. Nancy nodded to the judge and offered a weak smile.

"Yes, I have your honor," Mr. Lewis said.

"Good. I understand you are prepared to take your mother back to California with you Ms. Meyers."

"Yes."

"Your honor—her daughter has found a home for Mrs. Meyers." He handed over a document, which he had prepared. Judge Coates examined it.

"As soon as I'm gone, they'll make more seniors homeless!" Mildred said.

The courtroom exploded in applause. The reaction took Mildred by surprise. She turned around and pumped a power fist into the air. "Power to the people!" she shouted. Laughter and cheers erupted. The judge banged his gavel and glared angrily at Mildred.

"Order in the court!" It quieted the crowd. Nancy and Mr. Lewis tried to restrain Mildred.

However, she persisted. "I'm not leaving New York. We'll take our fight to Washington. To the supreme court—if we have to!"

"Mrs. Meyers, I'm on the verge of adding contempt of court to this already long list of charges." He took a moment to let it sink in. "I'm afraid you don't understand the seriousness of these charges. You won't be taking anything further than the Women's House of Detention where you spent the night, or someplace worse—if you don't go to California with your daughter."

"Well that's fine with me. From what I've seen so far, that place can use some rehabilitating, too!"

"Mom, please!"

"Your honor, may I have a moment to speak with my client."

"Yes!" The judge looked at his watch then out at the throng of people in his courtroom. "Please make it quick. I have a full docket this morning."

CHAPTER 10

The usual smoggy haze sat over the city of Los Angeles. Nancy's little white Mercedes 450SL slowly made its way through Hollywood morning traffic. Mildred gazed out the window, not impressed with L.A., and especially not Hollywood. She was still unhappy about having to leave New York, but she had to admit that it was better than going to jail. Nancy and Mr. Lewis had convinced her to take L.A. over a stiff jail sentence. Mildred turned to Nancy and said, "I always wanted to live in Hawaii."

"You did not. I remember growing up—you always said, 'It's a big world out there, but there's no place like New York.'"

"I said that?"

"Yes. You've only been to Hawaii twice. You don't know anything about living there."

"What's to know? You find a place to live, you make some friends, you find a synagogue, you do some shopping, you eat, you sleep, and the weather is warm all the time. What else is there?"

"It's warm here too."

"I'll grant you that. The cold was getting to me back there."

"See? Ma, you don't have any choice. The judge put you in my custody. I can get in trouble too."

Mildred's frustrated expression said it all. "He's in New York. How's he going to know whose custody I'm in?"

"He said they're going to check on you."

"Custody, custody… I'm sick of it already."

"Ma, at least give this place a chance. The people are very nice. Stanley, the guy who runs it, is too."

Nancy stopped for a light and sighed softly. Mildred stared out the window absent-mindedly. "How many times do you think you have to go someplace to know whether you like it?"

Somewhat exasperated, Nancy snapped, "You just can't go off to Hawaii by yourself and that's final. I don't want to hear anything else about it!" Nancy felt awful the moment the words came out of her mouth. She would not look over at her mother. Mildred appeared hurt by Nancy's harsh words. Nancy stopped for another light.

Under her breath, Mildred said, "Why all the fuss about where I want to live?"

The light changed and the car accelerated. "When I get back from this tour, we'll go together and look around. How does that sound?" Mildred sat silently staring ahead. Nancy glanced over at her then said, "It's a very expensive place to live."

"So's New York and Los Angeles. I know how to stretch my dollar."

Nancy's car pulled up in front of Star Bright. With tightly closed lips and a hurt, unhappy expression on her face, Mildred wouldn't look at her daughter or the house. She clenched her purse tightly on her lap.

"This is a very busy time for Jeff and me. Once we get this TV special on the air, I can spend more time with you," Nancy said.

Mildred wasn't budging.

"I just want you to be happy and have a nice place to live with some companionship."

"I had a nice place to live, until that Daniels guy tore it down," Mildred said this without looking at Nancy.

"Ma, what do you say? Will you at least stay until I come back?"

"I never thought this would happen to me. An old age home…"

"It's not that kind of place. Can you please just try it for a little while?"

Mildred thought for a moment, looked over at her daughter, and said, "All right, I'll look around but I'm not promising anything."

Inside Stanley's office, Mildred sat next to Nancy on the bench opposite Stanley's desk, her purse across her lap. Stanley sat behind his desk. "What about your mother and father?" Mildred asked.

"They're both dead. My father passed away about ten years ago from a heart attack." He turned around a picture sitting on his desk. It was his parents on their wedding day.

"That's a nice picture." Mildred appeared more at ease and warming to Stanley.

"My mother died about two years ago. She had cancer." He said it with a pained expression.

"I'm sorry to hear that. You have any brothers or sisters?"

"A brother who's a lawyer in North Carolina. I miss my Mom. After she died, I wished I had spent more time with her."

Mildred gave her daughter a see-I-told-you-so look. Nancy's face registered the barb.

Stanley sneezed twice.

"Bless you," Nancy said.

"Yes, God bless you. You have a cold?" Mildred asked.

"It's just my allergies. I get this way when the Santa Anas blow."

Mildred looked blankly at Stanley.

"It's the winds, Ma. When they blow off the desert."

"Oh." Mildred opened her purse looking for something. She removed a pill bottle, opened it, and shook out some tablets. She handed them to Stanley. "Here, take these! They always work for me."

Mildred got up and put them in Stanley's outstretched hand. He looked curiously at them "What are they?"

"It's an allergy medication. My doctor gave them to me years ago. You can't get them anymore. I get them from a guy on Canal Street. Even if you're coming down with a cold, they work. You got some water?"

"No, I don't."

"I'll get you some. Where's the kitchen?"

"Oh, just down the hall to the right. I'll go!"

"I'll find it."

Before Stanley could say anything else, Mildred walked out of the room, carrying her purse.

Nancy shrugged and said apologetically, "You can't stop her. That's just the way she is."

"She's cute. You think she'll stay?"

"I don't know. I sure hope so. I don't know what else to do with her. I think she's taken a liking to you."

Mildred entered the kitchen. Mrs. Watanabe, a Japanese woman in her late forties about the same height as Mildred, washed spinach in the sink. As a youngster, she and her family lived out World War II at the Manzanar Internment Camp in the high desert north of Los Angeles. She looked up as Mildred walked towards the sink.

"Oh, hello! Can I help you?" Mrs. Watanabe asked.

"I came to get some water for Stanley."

"You must be the new woman who's moving in."

"Well, I don't know if I'm staying."

"Oh?"

Looking around, she said, "This is a nice big kitchen."

"Yes. It is. I'm Sue, the cook. Stanley mentioned you were coming."

"I'm Mildred." Mrs. Watanabe extended her hand and they shook. "I need a glass and some water for Stanley."

Mrs. Watanabe wondered why Stanley didn't come and get his own water. She reached into one of the cabinets next to the sink and removed a glass. As Mildred walked to the sink, the cook handed her the glass. Mrs. Watanabe moved the spinach she was cleaning so Mildred could get some water.

"I just soak mine." Mildred turned the water off when the glass was full.

Mrs. Watanabe looked a little confused at first, then said, "Oh! Yes, that never seems to get all the dirt out."

"You probably just don't soak it long enough," Mildred said, smiling.

Mrs. Watanabe nodded unconvincingly. Mildred looked around the kitchen, admiring to herself how much larger it was than what she had in New York; hers was barely bigger than a closet. Before leaving, she gazed at Mrs. Watanabe rinsing a handful of spinach at a time, and Mildred walked out, shaking her head disapprovingly. It was already obvious the two women had differing opinions.

After Mildred returned to the office, Stanley swallowed the pills and took the women upstairs to see Mildred's room. He opened the door and let them go in first. The room had bright light coming from two windows facing the street. It had a bed with a mahogany headboard, a night table, and tall dresser opposite the foot of the bed. In between the windows sat an old comfortable armchair with a small table and a reading lamp on one side of it. Mildred walked around the room sizing it up. "It's nice. Isn't it Mom?" Nancy asked hopefully. She received no response from Mildred.

Stanley, sensing the tension between the women, offered, "Privacy is sacred around here. Nobody enters anyone else's room without permission." That seemed to strike a positive reaction on Mildred's part. "Do you mind being alone?" Stanley asked.

"No, of course not, I've lived by myself ever since Nancy left."

"I like to ask because some people like a roommate. Miss Louise and Mrs. Bennetti share one of the larger rooms. Mr. Kulak has his room. The Benson's theirs."

"Is there a synagogue in the neighborhood?"

Stanley's face beamed. "Right at the corner. You can walk there."

"What do you think Ma? You like the room?"

"It's a little smaller than I'm used to but that big kitchen makes up for it."

Stanley looked a little concerned about that last statement. "Well that's Mrs. Watanabe's domain." He quickly changed the subject and said, "Let me show you the backyard."

They walked out the back door from the kitchen into the yard that had some small pine trees and a large eucalyptus tree shading the rear of the small grassy yard. Miss Louis, an elderly woman in her seventies, thin with blond hair that had a hint of blue, sat in a lounge chair reading *Variety*. They walked over to her. Miss Louise stood up. "Hi, Stanley." She looked at Nancy and seemed to remember her from her earlier visit. She smiled pleasantly and said, "This must be your mother."

"Yes."

Stanley made introductions. "Miss Louise is an actress," Stanley said.

"Well, not so much anymore. No one seems to have work for an elderly thespian like me." Louise Hart had moved from Texas to New York when she was nineteen to pursue her acting career. Her father, a wealthy oilman, bought his daughter a ticket and gave her a stake to live on. She loved Shakespeare; her first Broadway production was in Shakespeare's *Twelfth Night*, shortly after she got to New York. It was the first opportunity of a successful career, which eventually led her to Hollywood and film work.

Miss Louise graciously extended her hand to Mildred and the women shook. "Please call me Louise. Are you staying with us?"

"I don't know yet?"

"I understand you come from New York. How is it these days? I haven't been there in years. I used to work a lot on Broadway back in the day. I miss New York, especially the Stage Deli and the wonderful apple strudel they made."

"New York's fine. I'm going to miss it. But not the cold winters. So you like strudel?"

"Oh, I love it."

"I'll make you some."

"Oh, you make strudel—how nice. That would be wonderful."

Mildred gazed around the yard. She turned to Stanley. "This is a nice big yard. No vegetable garden?"

"We've talked about one but no one ever seems to have the time."

Miss Louise touched Stanley's arm and asked, "Have there been any calls?"

"No, I'm sorry there haven't been."

Miss Louise said confidentially to the women, "My agent is working on something for me. A deal with Universal for a recurring role on a TV show."

Nancy and Mildred looked impressed and smiled.

"I want to introduce Mrs. Meyers to the others," Stanley said.

"Oh, they're watching the game shows. Nice to meet you Mildred. I hope you decide to stay with us. I think you'll like it here."

"Thank you, Louise. It was nice meetin' you."

"I love your New York accent."

"Accent? What accent?" Mildred asked.

Sunshine filtered through the front windows, giving the living room and with its old but well-kept furniture a bright, pleasant, and homey appearance. An upright piano stood against one of the walls. Stanley entered with the two women. Everyone present stared at the color TV opposite the couch. A re-run of an older game show played on the TV. Mr. Arthur Kulak, a lanky, mostly bald eighty-year-old, wore a black, form-fitting t-shirt and tight-fitting blue jeans; he sat in a chair next to the couch. He looked a lot younger than his years. He was a history teacher and school principal as well as a published author with books about world history, the Depression, and World War I.

From the TV, the host asked, "What cabinet position did Theodore Roosevelt hold prior to becoming president of the United States?"

Mr. Kulak said, "She doesn't know the answer."

The Bensons sat on the couch. Jim Benson, a robust man in his seventies, sat next to his wife. Mrs. Benson, a stocky woman about the same age as her husband, stared at the TV. The Bensons were the newest members of the house. They moved in about a year before and had previously lived in a much larger facility but didn't like it. They moved to Los Angeles from the Midwest.

Mrs. Benson spoke out of the side of her mouth in

a matter-of-fact sort of way, “What do you think it is, Arthur?”

“He was Secretary of the Navy,” Mr. Kulak said confidently.

They all looked away from the television as Stanley and his guests entered. Mildred immediately recognized the show and asked, “How much does she have?” They all turned in her direction. Mildred looked intently at the screen and sat down next to the Bensons. “She has four thousand and she’s going for five,” Mr. Benson said. Nancy and Stanley looked amused.

On the game show, a woman’s voice answered, tentatively, “Secretary of State?”

“No! You idiot,” Mr. Kulak shouted at the screen.

The game show host cut in, “No, I’m sorry the answer is—the Secretary of the Navy.”

“See I told you,” Mr. Kulak said.

“Oh, look how disappointed she is,” Mrs. Benson chimed in.

“Pardon me, this is Mrs. Meyers.” Stanley interrupted. They all turned to look at Mildred. Stanley pointed to the Bensons and introduced them, and then he introduced Mr. Kulak.

Jim Benson, sitting next to Mildred, turned to her and extended his hand. “Jim.”

His wife reached across her husband to shake Mildred’s hand. “You can just call me, Pauline,” Mrs. Benson said.

“You can call me Mildred.”

“Oh, I had an Aunt Mildred. She was such a lovely woman,” Mrs. Benson said.

Mr. Kulak popped out of his chair to go over to Mildred. Stanley, uncertain about Kulak's intentions, quickly said to Mildred, "This is Mr. Kulak."

Kulak extended his hand. He had to bend his lanky frame to take Mildred's hand, but instead of shaking it, he turned it over, bent closer, and kissed the back of it. Mildred blushed. "You can call me Arthur," he said in a seductive tone.

Stanley thought, *oh, no he's going to scare her off.*

Stanley quickly said, "You didn't meet Nancy when she was here. This is Nancy, Mrs. Meyers' daughter."

Kulak gave Nancy a quick once over with his eyes. He must have approved because he took her hand and kissed it as well. He even lingered a little while longer than he did with Mildred. "Pleased to meet you," he said as he straightened up.

Mrs. Benson said, "We met your daughter when she was here the other day. She's so lovely and beautiful." Nancy blushed uncomfortably. "You're lucky to have such a nice daughter. And I understand, talented as well." She winked playfully at Nancy. "We'll have to come to one of your performances some time. We used to always go the ballet when we lived in Chicago."

"I'm going there in a few weeks to perform."

"We loved Chicago," Mrs. Benson said; her husband nodded in agreement.

"Well, you may see her on television soon," Mildred said.

They all looked to Nancy for an explanation. "We're working on putting a production of *Giselle* together for PBS. I don't know if it's going to happen yet. We're still trying to get the financing. We're keeping our fingers crossed. My boyfriend and me."

"Well, we'll certainly look forward to that."

Mrs. Benson asked, "Are you going to stay with us, Mildred?"

Nancy took the opportunity to answer, "My mother hasn't decided yet."

"It's very nice. I love the kitchen. The room needs some freshening up. I might stay."

Stanley and Nancy looked surprised. For once, Nancy felt hopeful her mother would stay.

CHAPTER 11

Later that night at dinner, Mildred sat at the dining room table with Stanley and the other residents. Mrs. Bennetti, a heavy-set woman in her late-sixties, sat next to Mildred. She was born Anna Stephano on a family farm in Avellino, Italy, around ninety miles east of Naples. She came to the states as a fourteen-year-old and worked as a seamstress in a Brooklyn dress factory until she married Dominic Bennetti at seventeen. Her husband was a nineteen-year-old carpenter with a knack for gambling. In the 1950s, Dominic's brothers moved to the San Fernando Valley and were building houses for veterans. Dominic picked up his family of two girls and a boy to join his brothers.

"You mean you play the ponies and go to the track every day?" Mildred asked.

"Well, sometimes, I don't go. When I don't have any money or when, I don't feel good. Then, I stay home. I babysit my grandchildren once a week, too. I never miss Mass on Sundays. I used to go everyday but I don't do that anymore," Mrs. Bennetti said.

"How many grandchildren do you have?" Mildred asked.

"Well, two here. Six all together. The rest are all over the place, Seattle, Arizona, Vermont."

"Do you see them often?"

"I try to visit, and they come here every once in a while."

"I wish I had grandchildren," Mildred said.

"Don't worry, you will someday," Mrs. Bennetti said.

"I hope I have some before I die. Well, I don't approve of gambling," Mildred said. "When I was in jail…" Everyone looked at her in shock. "I shared a cell with a woman who stabbed her bookie. He was trying to collect the money she owed. She was a degenerate gambler, too."

"There's nothing degenerate about me," Mrs. Bennetti said, looking a little offended.

"Wait a minute, wait…" Mr. Kulak paused. "You said you were in jail?"

"Yes, just before I came here." They all looked at her apprehensively.

"What the hell did you do?" Kulak asked.

"It wasn't the first time either." They all looked shocked. "They tore down my tenement." Then, Mildred related the events that led to her incarceration and her present situation.

"Goddamn! I love it. What did they do, Mildred?" Kulak asked.

"They were afraid of us, but we were outnumbered. I didn't protect my rear—that was my mistake. The cops were coming at us from two sides."

"That's how Napoleon lost the Battle of Waterloo. The Prussians attacked his flank from the east. He was trapped between the British and the Prussians," Mr. Kulak said.

"It was a futile effort to save our homes from the claws of Calvin Daniels. He's tearing down buildings all over the city and putting up condominiums that senior citizens can't even afford. I wouldn't be surprised if he doesn't have projects going on here. We were all arrested. Because of my age, the judge didn't want to put me behind bars, but I had to agree to come out here."

"Did anyone get hurt?" Miss Louise asked.

Mildred pointed to the healing scar on the right side of her face. "My face was little scraped-up from a cop's rough treatment. Some of our younger supporters got beat up pretty bad. But mostly the cop's egos were bruised. They were afraid to hurt us older people—especially since the press and TV news were there. They didn't want to be accused of police brutality towards seniors with the TV cameras on them."

"I've heard that a lot of those old buildings in New York have been reclassified as historic," Mr. Kulak said. "Why didn't you seek historic preservation?"

"We tried that. They wouldn't have it. They turned down multiple requests. You have to be in the right neighborhood for that. One that the city wants to preserve. Brand new condominiums jack up property values for the city and increase the city's tax base."

"Well, Mildred, I'm proud to know you. You put up a good fight, nevertheless!" Mr. Kulak said.

"Me too," Mrs. Benson added. The others, including Stanley, congratulated Mildred. Mr. Kulak clapped his hands loudly.

A little while later, Mildred and Mrs. Bennetti carried soiled dinner plates, silverware, and glasses into the kitchen while Mrs. Watanabe tidied-up. Noticing them, she said, "Just put them in the sink. I'll get them in the dishwasher."

Mildred said, "I'll wash them!"

"You don't have to. We have a dishwasher," Mrs. Watanabe said as the women placed everything in the sink.

"An electric one?" Mildred asked.

The women looked at her curiously. "Yes."

"I never had one. I've always heard they don't come clean," Mildred said innocently.

"Oh, that's nonsense—they come out clean," Mrs. Watanabe, answered. Mildred shrugged her shoulders.

As Mildred and Mrs. Bennetti left the kitchen, Bennetti turned to Mildred and said confidentially, "She doesn't like us interfering in the kitchen."

Mildred wondered *why they couldn't help* but didn't say anything. The two women sat down at the table.

Mr. Kulak said, "People believe Roosevelt got us out of the Depression with all his public works programs. That wasn't it at all. Many of them were failures. His primary objective was staying in office. He dished out federal funds for his social programs in order to acquire votes to get him re-elected."

"There you go slamming the Democrats again," Stanley said.

"I'm not slamming the Democrats, just Roosevelt. He wanted to be king. Four terms he had." Kulak shook his head disgustedly. Stanley waved a dismissive hand at Kulak.

Mildred asked the Benson's, "What kind of business were you in?"

"Real estate. We owned our own agency," Mr. Benson said.

"Oh, that must have been a good business," Mildred said.

"It was for years. We tried selling real estate in Los Angeles when we moved here. To be frank, we lost our bee-hinds when these younger people came into the business. They had no respect for their clients and none for older people like us. Our age and trusting natures weren't a good fit here. We lost a considerable amount of money and decided to get out of the real estate business for good."

"When we were in the Midwest, we based our business on trust," Mrs. Benson said with a hint of pride in her voice.

"When people have money the housing market booms," Mr. Kulak said.

Mr. Benson said, "It wasn't so much that. We trusted everyone, and they in turn trusted and respected us. It's not like that anymore. Everyone's chasing the quick buck."

"It was like that with acting, too. People trusted you would do a good job. If you worked hard, they'd give you a break. I used to work all the time—stage, movies, and eventually TV. Today, whether you have talent or not doesn't matter. And if you're my age, they won't even talk to you. But I haven't given up, yet." Miss Louise nodded, affirming her convictions.

"What about that casting couch? You been on it, hah?" Kulak asked, followed by a devious laugh.

"Not when I was younger, but I'd jump on one now for a part." She laughed mischievously.

"So Louise, what's the best advice you ever got as an actress?"

"Oh, I can't remember. But my friend, Jimmy Stewart, was asked that on the set once by a young actor. Jimmy said to the young man, 'Learn your lines!'"

"You know Jimmy Stewart?" Mildred asked

"Yes, he and Gloria, his wife, are friends."

"Is he as nice in person?" Mildred asked.

"He's the same as on the screen," Miss Louise answered. "He took it hard when his stepson was killed in Vietnam a few years ago."

"Oh, I didn't know that," Mildred said.

Mrs. Bennetti said, "It's a terrible thing when a parent loses a child."

"I know. It's very sad," Mildred said. "My daughter's husband gave his life over there too." They all looked sympathetically at Mildred. "They were only married six months. After that, I protested the war."

"It was an illegal war—just like Korea," Mr. Kulak said.

Mildred looked around the table for something to do. She stood, and with a napkin, started sweeping crumbs into her hand. Mrs. Benson noticed Mildred and said, "Sit down Mildred! Sue likes to clean up."

"I can't. I have to do something all the time."

"I'd still like to do something useful," Mr. Benson, said.

Reluctantly, Mildred sat back down. She turned to Mr. Benson and asked, "Well what about SCORE? They have it out here? You can probably get involved with them. They can always use good people with experience like yours." Mildred looked around the table and realized no one knew what she was talking about. Stanley excused himself, got up and went into the kitchen.

“They help people start businesses. They mentor them until things get going,” Mildred said.

“It sounds interesting. I don’t know if we have the time.”

Mildred looked at him curiously and wondered why they wouldn’t have the time.

“I just want to take it easy and enjoy the time I have left,” Mr. Benson continued. “These days Pauline and I enjoy not having to be somewhere on a schedule. We always had appointments to show listings. We were going all the time. But I admire what you did Mildred—taking on the city of New York like that.”

“I’m gonna win one of those big million-dollar lotteries,” Mrs. Bennetti said. “That’s what I want. I’m happy when one of my picks comes in at the track. I won a daily double for two-hundred dollars the other day. That’s my happiness.”

Mildred looked at Mrs. Bennetti with a disgruntled expression.

In the kitchen, Stanley searched the refrigerator for something while Mrs. Watanabe rinsed dishes and placed them in the dishwasher. Mildred entered and tossed the table dirt into the trash under the sink. She looked at Mrs. Watanabe and said, “Oh, I’ll help rinse them!”

Being polite, Mrs. Watanabe said, “Okay, thank you.” She stepped away from the sink to let Mildred take over. Stanley removed a large size Hershey bar with almonds from the refrigerator, broke off a chunk and returned to the dining room. Mildred rinsed dishes and handed them to Mrs. Watanabe who placed them in the machine. However, she was having trouble keeping up with Mildred. After a while, she stepped back and said, "You better do it yourself." She walked away and started to put the leftovers into containers. Mildred continued to load the washer.

In a few minutes, Mildred finished rinsing and filling the dishwasher. She looked around helplessly. Finally, she said, "I don't know how one of these works."

Mrs. Watanabe expressed her gratitude for the help, but still felt annoyed by it. She walked over to the dishwasher and said, "You never had a dishwasher?"

"No."

Mrs. Watanabe removed detergent from under the sink, put it in the machine, and started the washer. Mildred started to scrub the sink and countertop with a sponge and cleanser. Once again, Mrs. Watanabe felt the imposition and walked back to her leftovers and put them in the refrigerator, mumbling something in Japanese under her breath. "They won't need me around here much longer."

CHAPTER 12

Mildred was having a restless night; she felt the dirt in the room closing in on her as she tossed and turned. Finally, she switched on the lamp, sat up, and glanced around the room. She got out of bed and put her robe over her nightgown to go to the bathroom down the hall. She opened the door and peeked into the hallway. As she stepped quietly out of her room, an uncomfortable feeling fell over her. She couldn't tell what it was. She tiptoed down the hall towards the bathroom. Just before she reached the door, it swung open, startling her. Her eyes focused on a naked Mr. Kulak coming out and she screamed. He looked just as surprised: one hand went to his chest as he fell back against the door, trying to catch his breath; the other hand shot to his privates. Mildred froze. She didn't know where to look. As much as she didn't want to look down, that's exactly where her eyes went. Doors opened up and down the hall. Mrs. Benson peered into the hall; another door opened and Miss Louise and Mrs. Bennetti came out in their robes.

"What's going on?" Mrs. Benson asked as she stared through the darkness. Her voice startled Mildred, who covered her eyes and quickly turned away from Kulak.

"I'm sorry… I'm sorry…" Kulak said.

Miss Louise said, "It's just Arthur, Mildred."

"What is he doing naked?" Mildred asked.

"It's alright Mildred, he's a nudist," Miss Louise said.

"I was just going to the bathroom. I didn't expect to see anyone," Kulak said.

In his pajamas, a disheveled Stanley dragged himself up the stairs. He looked around, wondering what all the commotion was about. Mr. Benson joined the group. They all stared at Kulak. "What, you ladies never seen a naked man before?" Kulak asked indignantly.

"Yes, you," Mrs. Bennetti snapped back. "But Mildred's new. She probably never saw a naked man in the middle of the night. Am I right, Mildred?"

Mildred didn't know how to answer that. She couldn't recall the last time she had seen a naked man. She had a few boyfriends over the years, but they were a long time ago.

Stanley rubbed his eyes, looked down the hall, and asked, "What's going on?" As he pushed his way through the others, he found out for himself. He stared at Kulak who stood helplessly with his hands still on his crotch.

"I'm sorry Mildred. I thought I could make a quick run to the toilet. I couldn't find my robe," Kulak tried to explain.

"Mr. Kulak, I've asked you not to do that," Stanley scolded. Kulak's head hung shamefully." Where are your pajamas?"

Everyone started talking at once. "He always does this," Mrs. Bennetti said.

"Arthur, you should be ashamed," Mrs. Benson

said. "Mildred's new here. She didn't have to see you naked her first night."

Stanley stood among the old people. Kulak just wanted to go back to bed, but couldn't because his path was blocked.

"Mr. Kulak, how many times have I told you not to do this? I told you to put a robe on, or please wear your pajamas," Stanley said authoritatively.

"I hate pajamas; they bunch up on me during the night. I feel like I'm choking, and they make me sweat." Kulak looked at them with doleful eyes, then pleaded, "Can we all just go back to bed now?"

Stanley said, "I'm sorry you had to experience this Mrs. Meyers."

"I'm sorry too, Mildred," Kulak apologized.

Mildred was at a loss for words and just shook her head.

"Let's all go back to bed," Stanley said.

They all headed to their rooms. Miss Louise stayed behind and took Mildred's arm. Mr. Kulak made his way past the others. Miss Louise turned around and made a clicking sound with her mouth at Kulak's naked butt. She whispered in Mildred's ear, "The old fart still has a cute ass."

Unconsciously, Mildred turned to look down the hall at Kulak's rear. Embarrassed, she quickly turned away.

"I heard that," Mr. Kulak said as he turned into his room.

Miss Louise said, "I'll wait for you, Mildred!"

"You don't have to do that."

"We don't need any more excitement tonight."

Mildred went into the bathroom while Miss Louise stood guard in front of the door with her arms folded across her chest. Stanley staggered down the stairs, scratching his head and yawning.

CHAPTER 13

In the early morning, the street outside Star Bright looked deserted, except for an old-fashioned, white milk truck with a slopping front that lumbered up the street, and stopped in front of the house. A middle-aged, man in white pants and shirt, and wearing a white sea captain's hat with a black brim, got out of the truck carrying a metal rack filled with milk bottles. He whistled softly as he walked down the driveway towards the back of the house. At the back door, he opened an aluminum box sitting next to the door and pulled out empties, replacing them with fresh bottles of milk. When he finished, he walked back down the driveway, the empties clanging as he made his way to the truck. He got in and pulled away with grinding gears.

Inside the house, it was still dark. Upstairs, furniture dragged across the floor, followed by something crashing with a thud. Mildred's door was slightly ajar and the light from her room spilled into the hallway. She wore a kerchief wrapped around her head and gray soot covered the front of her dark-colored dress. She struggled to pull a dresser away from the wall. Her mattress and box spring were propped against the opposite wall, the nightstand and chair sat in the middle of the room, bedding covered the chair, and the window curtains sat in a pile on the floor. Stanley, half asleep, climbed the stairs, his hair standing on end, wearing pajamas, and a white robe with pictures of green marijuana leaves spaced inches apart. His moccasins scraped on the floor as he made his way over to Mildred's door and peeked in. A puzzled look came over him. "Mrs. Meyers, what's going on?"

"Oh, good morning Stanley," Mildred answered perkily. She picked up the bedding, walked to the door, and pushed it into Stanley's chest; he reflexively put his arms around the bundle. "These have to be washed." Before Stanley could question her, Mildred said, "This place is filthy. I couldn't sleep a wink. And then that stunt Arthur pulled…"

"I'm sorry about that. I'll have to have a talk with him." He glanced around the room and asked, "What are you doing, Mrs. Meyers?"

"A general cleaning!"

Stanley scrunched up his face. "A general cleaning? What's that?"

"It's what should have been done before I moved in." With a smirk on her face, she shook her head from side-to-side.

"But we have cleaning people to do that. I asked them to clean your room thoroughly."

Mildred leveled her gaze at Stanley and shook her head. "Well they're not doing a very good job, Stanley."

He searched for words, but Mildred quickly said, "Take those things down to the washing machine. Where can I find a vacuum? A bucket? Some ammonia? And rags?"

"In the pantry down in the kitchen... I wish you wouldn't do this."

She pushed past him, and from over her shoulder, she said, "Bring those things down with you." She seemed to bounce down the stairs.

Kulak, fully dressed, came out of his room, walked over to Stanley and looked in the room. "What's she doing in there?" he asked.

"Mrs. Meyers is doing a general cleaning." He and Stanley exchanged confused glances. "We need to talk later!"

Mrs. Watanabe unlocked the back door, took the milk bottles out of the box, and walked into the kitchen. She opened the refrigerator placed the milk inside, then removed a carton of eggs. The inside door to the kitchen flung open and Mildred entered. Her entrance startled Mrs. Watanabe, who turned around so quickly she almost dropped the eggs. "Oh—you scared me. You're an early riser."

"Stanley said I can find the vacuum and cleaning things down here."

Mrs. Watanabe wondered why Mildred was asking for cleaning things, and pointed to the pantry across the room. "In there." She turned back to the refrigerator, removed butter and bacon, and put them on the counter next to the stove. The kitchen was still dark and Mrs. Watanabe flicked on the overhead lights.

At the same time, Mildred pulled out the vacuum cleaner, mops, brooms, and several containers of cleaning materials.

"What are you doing, Mrs. Meyers?"

"Cleaning my room. It's filthy." Mildred gathered

all her stuff and headed for the door where she crashed into Stanley, carrying the laundry pile. He apologized. Even though he was already quite fond of Mildred, he began to question his judgment about taking her in.

"Good morning, Mrs. Watanabe."

"Good morning Stanley. It looks like your new resident is a little busy." Stanley nodded in her direction as Mrs. Watanabe went about preparing breakfast.

Mildred dragged everything up the stairs, Mrs. Bennetti, still dressed in her blue chenille robe and wearing Donald Duck Slippers, came out of her room. She had a puzzled expression when she looked in Mildred's room, and asked, "What in the world are you doing, Mildred?"

"I'm doing a general cleaning. I couldn't sleep all night with this filth."

"Oh, but we have cleaning people to do that." Mrs. Bennetti walked away shaking her head uncertainly, talking to herself as she went into the bathroom, she said, "I hope we're not going to have to start cleaning our own rooms now."

After breakfast, Mildred had Stanley filling a bucket of water in the kitchen sink, and Kulak pulling sponges and rags out of the pantry and handing them to her. As she turned to leave the kitchen, she said, "And hurry up you two, I want to get this done and go shopping."

Stanley and Kulak made a feeble attempt to move faster as Mildred went out the door.

A little while later, the two men helped scrub the walls. The Bensons stopped and peeked in the room. Mrs. Benson gave an approving look as if to say it looked cleaner. "Mildred!" Mrs. Benson said.

Mildred stopped scrubbing and turned her attention to the Bensons.

"I've been telling Stanley for months now that these rooms aren't being cleaned properly. Haven't I said that Stanley?" Mrs. Benson asked.

Stanley turned to look at her. "I'll have to have a talk with the cleaning people."

"The place can use a fresh coat of paint, inside and out. That's what it needs," Mr. Benson said.

"With a good scrubbing, these walls won't look so bad. Why pay a painter when you don't have to," Mildred said with a smile.

Miss Louise appeared in the doorway. "My God! You are doing a job on this room."

"Until I clean it myself, I don't feel right."

"If we're going for our walk, we better get going, dear," Mr. Benson said to his wife.

Mrs. Benson said, "We'll see you later, Mildred,"

"Tomorrow, I'll help you with your room."

A surprised Stanley turned away from the wall. He wasn't expecting to hear that.

"Okay," Mrs. Benson said hesitantly and left.

Miss Louise stared at what was going on. "I don't know, Mildred. I wouldn't want to clean my room," she said indignantly. "I detest domestic chores."

"That's got nothing to do with it. I'll be finished here in no time."

Miss Louise said, "And you put these two to work." She laughed. "I thought I saw it all last night," leveling her gaze at Kulak. "But now, I've seen everything." She laughed again.

"Oh, shut up and get to work," Mr. Kulak said. He turned to Mildred, who dipped her sponge into his pail, and said, "She never did a decent days work in her life."

Miss Louise took offense. "Hah!" She turned and left.

Mildred started to climb on a chair to reach a higher spot on the wall. "I'll get up there," Kulak said.

"Never mind, never mind," Stanley quickly interjected. "I'll get up there. That's all I need is one of you falling and breaking a hip or worse." He took Mildred's sponge, climbed on the chair, and scrubbed the upper reaches of the wall.

"Arthur and I will start to put the furniture back," Mildred said to Stanley. Kulak positioned himself at one end of the dresser and began to push while Mildred pulled.

CHAPTER 14

Later that afternoon, Stanley pushed a supermarket grocery cart down the baking goods aisle. He was having a difficult time keeping up with Mildred, who walked several feet ahead of him. As she whisked down the aisle, she grabbed things off the shelf, tossing them into the cart. She had to stop in front of the sugar because she couldn't get to the five-pound bags. A man crouched in front of the shelf. He had a five-pound bag in one hand and a smaller box of sugar in the other; he was comparing prices. He looked up at Mildred for help. Stanley caught up with Mildred and gawked at the man. The man said to Mildred, "I don't know what to buy. I don't need all this sugar but it's cheaper than this box."

Mildred looked curiously at him. He was handsome with thinning blond hair and streaks of gray-blond hair. "That's what they do. You're better off buying the big one. It doesn't go bad."

"But I don't need all this sugar."

"Yeah, well that's how they get you." She stared at him and thought she recognized him from somewhere. He smiled back.

Stanley whispered something in Mildred's ear. She looked bug-eyed at Stanley then the man. "You're Mclean Stevenson from *M*A*S*H*," Mildred said.

He stood up smiling, and he was tall. “Yeah, that’s me.”

“I love to watch your show.”

“Thank you. So you would recommend the big one?”

“I know it’s a shame.”

“It’ll take a couple of years for me to use it all. I don’t cook, and I just use a little in my coffee in the morning.”

“You can do what I do sometimes.”

“What’s that?”

“When I go into McDonald’s, I grab a couple of handfuls of those little packages.”

“I’ll have to try that. What’s your name?”

“Mildred… Mildred Meyers.”

“Nice to meet you Mildred.” He reached out and shook Mildred’s hand, then Stanley’s. “Is this your son?”

“Oh, no. I live in his house. I just moved here from New York. My daughter is a ballet dancer. She lives here.

“Oh, what’s her name?”

“Nancy Meyers.”

“I don’t think I know her. Well, thanks again for your help. I better get moving along. Good luck in L.A. It’s a tough city, but you’re from New York. You know what they say, ‘If you can make it in New York, you can make it anywhere.’”

“Thanks,” Mildred said.

He tucked the sugar under his arm and walked to the front of the store.

Mildred picked up a bag of sugar, and they continued down the aisle. "He was very nice. My first star."

"Well, not your first."

"I haven't met any others."

"Yes, you have."

Mildred had a bewildered look on her face.

"Miss Louise! She was your first. She had quite a career. She doesn't talk about it much but she worked with all the big ones, Bogart, Henry Fonda, Clark Gable…"

As they walked down the cleaning supplies aisle, Mildred snatching cleansers and cleaning products, she said, over her shoulder, "I don't know about that cleaning service you have. They're not cleaning thoroughly."

"I'll have to get after them."

Mildred said, "You should get rid of them. We can do the cleaning."

"I can't have you people cleaning. The others don't want to do that."

"I'll do the cleaning. You'll save a bundle of money. I can do a thorough job on the whole house in a few days."

While Mildred compared prices of two furniture polishes, Stanley said, "Let me think about it."

Mildred selected one of them and tossed it in the cart. "That should do it for now. What's to think about? If you have to think—it's settled. I'll clean."

They headed towards the checkouts. "I can't believe Mr. Kulak helped," Stanley said.

"After what he pulled last night, he must have felt guilty."

"Mrs. Meyers, you should have seen what he was like when he first moved in. He's so much better now. He went through a bad time after his wife died. I believe he was wracked with guilt and grief. Apparently, he wasn't a very good husband."

At the checkout, Mildred placed the contents of the carriage on the counter.

"They wanted me to throw him out after he had a hooker in his room," Stanley said.

"What? A hooker?" she asked a little too loud, and it attracted nearby shoppers' attention.

"I've had a lot of heart-to-heart talks with him. He trusts me and confides in me. You know he wrote a high school textbook about the Roman Empire? He's very smart."

"Hmm…"

The cashier rang up their order and put it in bags. Stanley took out cash to pay but Mildred pushed his money away. "I got this one."

"No, I can't let you do that." The cashier looked annoyed by their bickering and just wanted to complete the transaction. Mildred handed her a hundred dollar bill.

"Mrs. Meyers, you can't be paying for things too."

"If I couldn't do it, I wouldn't." The cashier handed Mildred her change and was ready to move onto the next customer. Stanley picked the bags off the counter. "I'll take one of them," Mildred said. They struggled over the bags for a moment while the cashier looked on impatiently.

Finally, Stanley said, "I got them." They walked out the front door.

CHAPTER 15

When Stanley and Mildred arrived at Star Bright, Miss Louise and the Bensons were sitting on the front porch. Miss Louise noticed Stanley carrying the bags. "You bought a lot," she said.

"Oh, it's not so much. I'm going to make something special," Mildred said with a wink and a mischievous smile. She was excited about doing something nice for everyone.

Stanley sensed the Bensons and Miss Louise had something on their minds. But before he could ask, Mrs. Benson said, "We better tell him." Her husband and Miss Louise nodded in agreement.

"There was a man here. He said he was from the licensing commission?"

Stanley looked puzzled. "The licensing commission? What do they want?"

Disgustedly, Mrs. Benson said, "He was snooping around taking notes."

"He left this." Mr. Benson said and handed Stanley a yellow sheet of paper with a business card attached. Stanley glanced over it with a frown.

"That isn't all," Miss Louise said. Stanley looked at her expecting the worst. "Before he left, Arthur mooned him."

Mildred raised an eyebrow.

"Oh, no!" Stanley said.

Mildred chimed in, "What? I don't believe that. We were just talking about him." The others nodded that it was true.

CHAPTER 16

Later that night, Mrs. Bennetti, Mrs. Benson, Miss Louise stood in the kitchen with Mildred between them. Mildred wore an apron covered in flour with her glasses hanging from a chain and flour all over them. Bowls, baking utensils, and flattened rounds of dough sat on the counter in front of them. Mildred spread orange-colored filling on the rounds. The other women used spoons to smooth out the filling then sprinkled them with nuts, raisins, and cinnamon. "Now, we just have to roll them up," Mildred said.

Mrs. Watanabe put on her sweater and walked to the door. She stopped to look back at what the women were doing. "Please don't leave me with a mess in the morning."

"Don't worry. We'll clean up. Goodnight!" Mildred said. The others wished her a good night.

"Goodnight," Mrs. Watanabe said and left.

Mildred placed each of the strudels on a baking sheet, took them to the oven, opened the door, and placed them inside.

After forty-five minutes, Mildred removed the golden-browned strudels from the oven.

"They look beautiful, Mildred," Mrs. Bennetti said.

"They sure do Mildred," Mrs. Benson added.

Miss Louise smiled and said, "The aroma is making my mouth water."

As Mildred carried the tray over to the counter, she said, "Pauline can you put the coffee on and some water for tea."

"Sure."

"Now, we just have to let them cool, and then we can sprinkle them with powdered sugar."

Mildred called Stanley and he appeared in the doorway. "Hmm… What smells so good?"

"Strudel!"

Stanley went over to the counter to ogle the strudel.

"Ask the men to come into the dining room in a few minutes. Pauline is making coffee and tea. We'll bring everything out. Then we can talk about that stupid list," Mildred said.

They all sat around the dining table. Mildred entered, carrying a large platter of strudel cut into slices. Powdered sugar, resembling freshly fallen snow, covered the strudel. Mrs. Benson carried a tray with cups, a coffee pot, teapot, dessert plates, and forks.

"See that? She said she was going to make it and she did," Miss Louise said with a smile.

"Oh Mildred, it looks wonderful," Mrs. Benson said. Mildred puffed out her chest proudly.

"My wife used to make a pretty good strudel. She was a wonderful cook, too." Mr. Kulak said. The others looked at him, surprised because it was the first time he had spoken about her.

"Sit down Mildred! You must be exhausted. You've been going since early this morning," Mrs. Bennetti said.

"Oh, I'm fine. Besides, I have another one in the oven. It needs a few more minutes."

"Mildred, sit down right now!" Miss Louise commanded. "Stanley can go and check. Go ahead Stanley." The others chimed in, and Mildred reluctantly sat down. Stanley popped up and headed for the kitchen.

"Stanley, if it's browned, please take it out and put it on the counter," Mildred said.

"Okay."

"And please turn the oven off if it's done."

"Well I can't wait any longer," Mr. Kulak said, grabbing a piece of strudel and putting it on his plate. When he bit into it, his expression spoke for itself. "Delicious," he said, smacking his lips and taking a second bite.

They passed the plate around until everyone took a piece. With her mouth full, Mrs. Benson said, "Yum… Yum…"

Stanley returned. He looked over at Mildred. "I took it out."

"Thanks, Stanley! Now, sit down and have a piece."

Mildred watched Stanley take his first bite. With his mouth full, he said, "Mrs. Meyers this is delicious. I've never had apple strudel before."

"It tastes like apple, but it's not apple. I put golden raisins and apricot preserves."

"You had me fooled," Mr. Kulak said.

Mildred removed from her apron pocket the folded yellow paper. "About these violations… If we all pitch in, we can correct them. The rest is harassment, but that's beside the point." She looked around the table and everyone appeared agreeable. "Now, Stanley, Jim, Arthur, you can take care of the repairs. Louise, since you don't like cleaning, you can help Stanley shop for paint and the other things we need." Miss Louise nodded her approval. "Pauline, Anna and I…" She looked at Mrs. Bennetti. "Anna, can you stay home tomorrow?"

"Sure."

"Good. We'll take care of everything inside. Any questions?" She looked around the table; everyone was too busy eating to say anything. Mildred couldn't control the big yawn that came over her.

"You better get a good night's sleep, Mildred." Mildred nodded in Mrs. Bennetti's direction. "And you quit walking around naked," she said to Mr. Kulak. He bowed his head apologetically.

CHAPTER 17

The next morning, Mildred's room had a clean, fresh, and bright look about it. She was making her bed and there was a knock at the door. "Come in!

"Mildred, it's me, Pauline."

"It's open." Mildred realized Mrs. Benson couldn't hear her and walked over to open the door.

"Good morning," Mrs. Benson said.

"Good morning. Come in."

Mrs. Benson entered. "I had to get away for a few minutes. Jim's in bad spirits," she said confidentially from the side of her mouth. "His knee is bothering him. He won't tell me, but I know it. After fifty years of living with someone, you just know when something isn't right."

"Have him put a heating pad on."

"Oh, I'm sure that's what he is doing. It's just an old football injury. He's had a few operations on his knees but every once in a while they act up."

"Does he have pain killers?"

"Yes. The doctor told him to take them when the pain gets too bad. He doesn't like to. You know—they constipate you. When we were at the other place, they gave you all sorts of pills every day. They kept people alive with the pills and killed you with the food. Jim says it was better life through chemistry."

"It's nice here. I feel like I'm in my own home."

"You wouldn't like one of those big places. I hated it. And the people… Most were half-dead. You just have to watch out for that Kulak. He's a little unusual."

"Oh, I think he's just lonely."

"Well don't be surprised if you see him naked again. I tell you, he's a pervert. In his room, he has those nasty magazines everywhere. I wouldn't dare go in there. Well I better get back and see how Jim's doing. So I don't know how much help he will be today."

"You tell Jim not to worry and to rest if he has to. We'll manage somehow."

"Stanley and Louise left for the store already. I think they ate most of the strudel for breakfast." She touched Mildred's arm. "And it was wonderful."

"Thank you."

She left and Mildred finished straightening out.

CHAPTER 18

Stanley and Miss Louise carried in bags and boxes from the hardware store. Mildred and Kulak moved furniture from the living room into the dining room where the table was up against the wall. Mrs. Bennetti removed the drapes from the windows and put them in a pile on the floor. Mr. and Mrs. Benson came down the stairs into the living room. He walked with a slight limp. Mildred noticed them and said, "How are you feeling, Jim?"

"Much better! Thank you. I'm ready to pitch-in. What can I do?"

Stanley put down the last of the supplies and asked, "You want to work on the windows?"

"Sure."

"There's putty and a gun in the bag. Can you scrape the old putty and put new around the outside windows?"

"Sure."

"But I don't want you on the ladder. Call me to do anything on top."

Mr. Benson removed a putty gun, a tube of putty, and some tools and went outside. Mrs. Benson looked to Mildred for direction. Mildred responded, "You can help Louise and Anna with the drapes. Then, we have to clean the windows inside and out."

Mrs. Benson went over to help Mrs. Bennetti who wobbled a little carrying the large bundle of drapes into the kitchen. They collided with Mrs. Watanabe who opened the door to peek into the room.

Mildred noticed Mrs. Watanabe and asked, “All through in the kitchen?”

Mrs. Watanabe said, “Oh Mildred the strudel was delicious. You’ll have to give me the recipe,” and she returned to the kitchen.

Mrs. Benson followed Mrs. Watanabe into the kitchen, leaving Mrs. Bennetti standing at the door.

Mildred said to Mrs. Bennetti, “See if Sue needs any help in the kitchen.”

CHAPTER 19

Inside the San Francisco Opera House, a rehearsal of Swan Lake was concluding. Nancy, Karen, and the other dancers twirled and pirouetted to Tchaikovsky's score. Nancy gracefully performed the final movements of the ballet as the orchestra built to a crescendo and the music stopped. The dancers froze in their places. The director shouted from the rear of the theatre, "Very nice. I'm satisfied. Get some rest and be back here at seven."

Everyone broke for the wings. A handsome, young, well-built Italian dancer, who looked more like a weight lifter then a ballet dancer, walked alongside Nancy and Karen. He flipped his black hair away from his dreamy blue eyes.

"You want to come shopping with me?" Karen asked Nancy.

Nancy smiled at the young man. "Thanks, but Michael and I have plans."

"Okay. I'll see you tonight." Karen ran ahead to the dressing room while Michael and Nancy held a passionate gaze.

Later in Nancy's San Francisco hotel room, Michael and Nancy tossed around naked in bed, making love. When they finished, Nancy's cheeks were red and hot with lust. Michael rolled over on his back. The two of them sat propped up by pillows. "That wassa nice," Michael said with a slight Italian accent.

"Yeah, you think so?"

Michael looked a little put off by the question. "Whatta you mean?" he said with hurt in his voice.

Nancy smiled at him and put a hand on his cheek, then kissed him gently on his other cheek. "I'm just kidding. It was wonderful. You make me feel so good."

"Oh, *gracie, mi amore*." Michael picked up a small vial from the night table, opened it and put a little of its white powder on the night table, wetting his finger with the tip of his tongue, he dabbed it into the powder, then offered it to Nancy. She shook her head, refusing.

"You shouldn't do that stuff."

"Aa, ittsa only a little for the pain."

"That's what happens. You do a little, then a little more, and before you know it you're doing it all day long, every day." He ignored her and sniffed the cocaine. "I spent a month in rehab to kick my habit."

"I be all right. You don't worry *mi amore,* just a little now and then for a the pain."

"Yeah, that's what you say now. You can lose your job too if they catch you high."

"Not to worry."

Nancy frowned. "Just be careful… I better call my mother and see how she's doing."

"You momma—she's a sick?"

"No, no. She just moved into a new place." She leaned across Michael, picked up the phone and dialed.

CHAPTER 20

Stanley's office furniture sat on the front porch. Mr. Kulak was out there tightening the hinges on the screen door with a screwdriver. Mr. Benson scraped old flakey, loose putty from around one of the front windows. Then he applied new putty around one side of the window. He put his putty gun down and, not realizing, he began to remove the fresh putty that he just applied to the other side of the windows. "Oh, gosh, darn," he mumbled to himself, looking around to see if anyone noticed his mistake. Only Kulak was there and he was too busy to notice.

In the kitchen, Mrs. Watanabe stood on the countertop, removed dishes from the top of the cabinet, and handed them to Mrs. Bennetti, who placed them on the counter.

Out in the hallway, Mrs. Benson stood on a stepladder screwing a bulb into the light fixture while Mildred busied herself on the stairs stapling loose carpet treads. Mrs. Benson said, "That Louise and her acting jobs. She'll drive you crazy. She hasn't worked in years."

Mildred turned to look at Mrs. Benson. "You told me that. But she said something about a contract, and Stanley said she was quite a movie star."

"Oh, it's just plain old talk. Don't believe it for one minute."

Just then, Stanley came out of his office dressed in khaki Carhartt work clothes. A panicky look came over him. "What are you doing up there?"

He startled Mrs. Benson, who teetered a little on the ladder. Stanley rushed over to grab her. "Get down! Let me do that."

"I'm alright." But she teetered again when she turned to address Stanley. He quickly reached out to steady her. "Come down from there!" He held her around the waist until her feet touched the floor.

"You worry too much, my dear."

"Never mind. I don't want any of you on ladders. Call me to do anything that involves a ladder."

Stanley went outside and removed a broken piece of concrete from in front of the steps.

Miss Louise came down the driveway pulling a hose. "Here! I'll go back and turn it on."

Stanley took the hose and she left. A minute later, water came spurting out. Stanley sprayed it into a pile of sand and cement on the ground at his side. He put the hose down and mixed the cement with a shovel. Inside, the telephone rang in his office. Mrs. Benson called out. "Oh—oh… Stanley!

All of a sudden, there was a lot of confusion as Stanley, Kulak, and Mr. Benson all rushed to the front door. Finally, Stanley said. "I'll get it—I'll get it!" He went inside and as he got to his office door, he collided with Mildred and Mrs. Benson also trying to get to the phone. "I'll get it," he said to them. He went in grabbed the phone mid-ring, and breathlessly answered, "Hello, Star Bright Senior Residence, this is Stanley."

"Oh hi, Stanley. It's Nancy Meyers," the voice at the other end responded.

"Hi Nancy." At the mention of her daughter's name, Mildred's ears perked up.

"Oh, I think it's your daughter," Mrs. Benson said.

Mildred gave her a look and said, "I know."

"How are you?" Nancy asked.

"I'm fine. We're busy making some repairs and cleaning up around here."

"I knew my mother would get around to something like that."

"No. We have to comply with some city regulations."

"So, how's my mother doing?"

"She's fine. She's right here. Let me put her on. So long." He handed the phone to Mildred who anxiously stood in front of his desk.

First thing out of Mildred's mouth: "What's the matter?"

"Nothing. I just called to see how you're doing."

Stanley and the others stood by the door listening. Stanley said, "Let's get out so Mrs. Meyers can talk." They left the room.

"Don't talk too long—it's expensive," Mildred said over the phone.

"Ma, don't worry about it. I have an expense account."

"Oh. They pay for it?"

"Yes," Nancy said a little impatiently.

"I hope you're eating well and taking you're vitamins." Nancy in the past had suffered from anorexia and bulimia. It was a constant worry for Mildred. She didn't want to see her daughter in rehab again.

“Ma, I’m fine. I just ate a big lunch. How do you like it there?”

“I’m settling in. Everyone is very nice.”

“That’s good. You miss New York?”

“Sure, I miss New York. But not that cold weather. The days are so nice here.” An awkward silence followed, which often occurs with conversations between children and parents.

Finally, Mildred asked, “So how’s your knees?”

“They’re pretty good. I’m been icing them before and after rehearsals and shows.”

“Use your heating pad too.”

“The doctor said to just ice them. I take two aspirin, a hot bath and a glass of sherry before going to the theatre.”

“The heating pad is better. How many shows are you doing?”

“We do one each night, then matinees on Saturday and Sunday. We’re off on Mondays.”

“Hmm… I hope it’s not going to be too much for your knees.”

“I’ll be alright, Mom. I’m not going to be doing this much longer. I’ve been interviewing for choreographer positions.”

“You didn’t tell me about that.”

“I guess I forgot with moving you out here and everything. Ma, I’m thirty-three. I can’t keep dancing much longer. But it will be a big change.”

“I know sweetheart. I hope you will be happy doing that.”

“I think I will. What the heck, I have to try.”

“Well you better get off the phone. It’s expensive.”

“I told you they pay for it.”

"Yeah, but they probably don't like you running up big phone bills. I'll say goodbye. Thank you for calling."

Nancy chuckled a little. "Okay Mom, goodbye."

"And take your vitamins. And don't forget to put the heating pad on."

With exasperation in her voice and feeling like a little girl again, she said, "Yes, Mom. I take them every morning. I'm going to put the heating pad on right now. Take care of yourself. I'll call in a few days. I love you."

"I love you too. Bye." Mildred hung up the phone.

She walked back into the hall where Stanley and Mrs. Benson stood. They noticed the glow on her face.

"Is everything alright with your daughter?" Mrs. Benson asked.

"She sounds good. They do six nighttime shows and two matinees on the weekend. They're off on Monday."

Stanley smiled, "I saw her and Karen dance once. She's very good."

Mildred said, "I know. Her lessons cost me enough. You know she studied in Nice for a while with a very famous ballet artist. I forget his name, but he was a famous one."

Stanley and Mrs. Benson looked extremely impressed. Mildred puffed her chest out proudly. "Well, let's get back to work!"

CHAPTER 21

The dining room table was set for dinner. Everyone but Mildred sat at the table. Mr. Benson and Mr. Kulak snoozed while Mrs. Bennetti knitted. An exhausted-looking Miss Louise listened to Stanley and Mrs. Benson as Stanley read over the list of violations. "Stanley, what about the smoke detectors?" Mrs. Benson asked.

"I'll put the new ones in tomorrow."

"And what about the weather-stripping on the front door?"

Stanley looked up from his list, and said, "All fixed."

"And the loose floor boards upstairs?"

Stanley asked, "Mr. Kulak!" Kulak eyes popped open. "Did you nail down those boards upstairs?"

Kulak snapped his fingers, "Good as new."

"Thank you."

In the kitchen, Mrs. Watanabe worked at the stove while Mildred still in her cleaning clothes made a salad. Mildred asked, "Do you have the corn in the pot?"

Mrs. Watanabe gave her an annoyed look. "Yes!"

Mildred walked over to the stove, lifted the cover and peered in. "I told you it was in the pot!"

"I'm just gonna turn it up a little." Mildred turned

the gas knob and increased the heat under the corn. Mrs. Watanabe threw Mildred a disparaging look. In defense, Mildred said, "It will cook faster."

"Who's cooking here?

"Well you're.... you're... too slow," Mildred accused. Mildred opened the oven door and checked the roasting chickens. Mrs. Watanabe gave Mildred a sideways glance from the other side of the room. Mildred was oblivious to it and returned to her salad. She sprinkled salt, pepper and tossed the salad with dressing, then took it out to the dining room and quickly returned. When Mildred returned, she saw Mrs. Watanabe at the stove, stirring the corn. Mildred picked up a serving dish and brought it over.

"What are you doing?" Mrs. Watanabe asked.

"It looks ready." Mildred tried to pick up the pot, but Mrs. Watanabe wouldn't let her. "Come on. We haven't got all night. Everyone's hungry and tired. Let's get some food on the table!"

Mrs. Watanabe released the pot; Mildred dumped its contents into the serving bowl. She opened the oven door again, looked in, and closed the door. Picking up the corn, she headed for the dining room. Over her shoulder, she ordered, "Bring the chicken out! It's ready." Mrs. Watanabe made a face, mumbled something to herself in Japanese, and stood with her hands on her hips as Mildred went out the door. When Mildred returned, she looked around for the chicken. "Didn't you take the chicken out?"

Mrs. Watanabe picked the empty corn pot off the stove. "I don't like to be rushed like this."

Mildred backed away because it looked as though Mrs. Watanabe wanted to strike Mildred with the pot, but she put it in the sink instead.

"If you moved any slower, we'd be eating at midnight."

Mrs. Watanabe felt her anger mounting and said, "Oh yeah? I haven't heard any complaints yet. Just you. I don't like you interfering in my kitchen."

"Oh, excuse me. I didn't know the kitchen belonged to you."

In the dining room, the two women arguing in the kitchen woke a snoozing Mr. Benson. Everyone sitting around the table turned their attention to the closed kitchen door and the commotion coming from there. They heard Mildred shout back, "You move like a snail!" Stanley looked ashen as he got up and went in the kitchen where Mrs. Watanabe and Mildred were in a face off, their faces only inches apart. "You're a crazy person!"

Stanley stepped between them. "Now, hold it a minute! What's going on here?"

Mildred snapped, "Everyone's tired and hungry. She don't care when we eat."

"If she doesn't stay out of this kitchen, I'm leaving. I don't do anything right, according to Miss Betty Crocker."

"Alright, alright, please calm down both of you. Is everything ready?"

Under her breath, Mildred said, "It's probably burnt by now."

Stanley shot Mildred a pleading look. "Please, Mrs. Meyers…"

"Yes, it is ready," Mrs. Watanabe, answered.

"Mrs. Meyers, please let Mrs. Watanabe do her job." He gently took Mildred's arm and led her towards the door. "Come and sit down." He turned to the cook, and said, "Mrs. Watanabe please bring everything out as soon as you're ready."

As Stanley and Mildred left the room, Mildred said, "She wants to leave, let her."

Calmly, Stanley said, "Shh…"

Mrs. Watanabe opened the oven door and removed the chicken.

In the dining room, Mildred said, "Let her leave! She puts so much salt in everything; she's going to give somebody a heart attack." The others sat quietly around the table with concerned looks as they watched Mildred take her seat with a huff. Stanley sat down too.

A few moments later, Mrs. Watanabe came in and placed a platter of chicken on the table. Sensing the cook's distress, Stanley said, "Mrs. Watanabe, it's getting late. Why don't you leave early tonight? We can clean up."

The woman just nodded and left the room without a word. A silence fell over the table as they passed the food around. Stanley tried to make light of the situation and said cheerfully, "Alright, let's eat!"

CHAPTER 22

Mildred wore sandals, a cotton dress, and a straw hat with a brim around it while she cleared grass from a ten-foot by five-foot plot—a spot covered in sunshine. Miss Louise sat nearby in a lawn chair reading *Variety*. Pulled grass sat in a pile at Mildred's side. She turned over the rich, brown soil and raked it smooth. Mrs. Watanabe came out the kitchen door carrying a plastic bag with trash; she and Mildred exchanged unfriendly glances. Mrs. Watanabe quickly dumped the trash in the can and went inside. Mildred continued raking. "Why can't you just go in and apply for a job?" she asked Miss Louise.

"It's doesn't work that way. There are too many actors around. The casting people won't even talk to you unless an agent sets up an appointment. It wasn't like that in the old days. We were all under contract so they felt obligated to put you to work."

"Well—I don't understand that. How are people supposed to get work?"

The Bensons came out the back door. "Oh, you've made a lot of progress, Mildred," Mr. Benson said.

Louise and Mildred looked at the Bensons as they walked over to the future garden.

"Do you think the soil is good enough to grow anything?" Mrs. Benson asked.

Mildred reached down and grabbed a handful and said, "It looks very healthy to me."

"Oh, I think you are right Mildred," Mr. Benson said, as he took a pinch from Mildred's hand and smelled it.

"What are you going to plant?" Mrs. Benson asked.

"Some tomatoes, lettuce, squash, spinach… maybe some herbs, too. Fresh herbs are always nice to have in your cooking."

The Bensons smiled. "It will be so nice to eat fresh-picked produce instead of that store bought stuff," Mrs. Benson said.

"Going for a walk?" Mildred asked.

Mr. Benson looked up at the sky and replied, "It's a lovely day for one. We better get going dear."

"Oh, yes," Mrs. Benson said. Mr. Benson tossed the dirt between his fingers back on the ground.

"Have a nice walk," Miss Louise said.

"Thank you. We'll see you in a little while," Mr. Benson said. He turned around and with his first few steps, a pained expression came over his face. The three women exchanged sympathetic gazes.

"Bye!" Mildred said. Mrs. Benson looped her arm in her husband's as they walked out of the yard. The other two watched Mr. Benson limp down the driveway.

Miss Louise said, "His knee must be bothering him."

"She said it was bothering him this week." Mildred put her rake down and picked up the shovel.

"God bless them. They never miss their walk." Miss Louise lowered her voice to a confidential tone. "You know, they sneak off to their room in the afternoon." Mildred looked at her with a blank expression. "I think they still do it."

Mildred blushed. "Oh! You think so?" Miss Louise gave her a confirming wink.

Mrs. Bennetti came out the back door wearing a Hollywood Park cap with binoculars hanging around her neck and carrying her tote with racing forms, newspapers, and knitting sticking out the top. Mildred noticed the knitting and asked, "What are you knitting?"

"A sweater for my granddaughter."

"I'll have to lend you some of my patterns."

"I would love that. I always make the same ones. It would be nice to try something new. Well, I'm off to the track." Mildred and Louise looked at her. "Wish me luck!"

Mildred returned Mrs. Bennetti's enthusiasm with an admonishing look.

"Want me to make any bets for you? I got a hot tip yesterday from one of the groomers—Double Play in the sixth race, today," Mrs. Bennetti said.

"Stay home— that's the best bet," Mildred said.

Mrs. Bennetti laughed. "You're a hoot Mildred. I better get going before I miss my bus. If you miss a bus here it's not like New York, you wait forever. And at our age, that's not a good thing." She laughed again. "I could die at one of those bus stops."

"Believe me you have to wait forever in New York, too," Mildred said.

"Dominic, my husband, used to say they have only one bus in L.A. Sometimes, I think he was right." She raised her wrist in front of her thick glasses and stared at her large-numbered watch. "Well, I better be going. So long." She scooted out of the yard.

"Good luck, Anna," Miss Louise shouted after her.

"Thank you," Mrs. Bennetti said over her shoulder.

"Be careful with your money!" Mildred added. She turned her attention back to her plot of land and started to make troughs for seeds. Miss Louise returned to reading her newspaper.

CHAPTER 23

Stanley sat at his office desk, munching corn chips from an opened bag sitting on the desk next to an opened can of Coke. The door to one of the display cases behind him was ajar. Several toy soldiers from the case stood on the desk facing Stanley. In between eating the chips and sipping his Coke, he carefully cleaned each soldier with a small, soft white cloth and a toothbrush. A knock on the office door made him look up. A serious-looking middle-aged man, wearing wire-rimmed glasses and a three-piece black suit, stood in the doorway. "I'm Mr. Forman from the licensing commission. I was here the other day."

"Oh yeah, they told me you were here."

Stanley stood up and extended his hand. "I'm the owner, Stanley… Stanley Cutler." They shook hands.

"When I was here, my inspection turned up a number of violations, Mr. Cutler."

"I know. We've taken care of them."

"You have?"

"Yes."

Mr. Kulak appeared in the doorway. Noticing Forman, he turned quickly and walked away. He scurried through the house and out the back door into the yard. "He's here!" he shouted to Mildred and Miss Louise. The two women looked at him.

"Who?" Mildred asked.

"That man from the licensing commission."

Mildred threw down her rake and the three of them headed for the kitchen door.

"And keep your pants on!" Miss Louise advised.

They squeezed into Stanley's office, surprising him and Mr. Forman. "These are some of my residents," Stanley said. He made introductions.

"Yes, I think I met some of you the other day." No one said anything, especially Kulak who avoided Forman's gaze.

"So how long have you been doing this kind of work, Mr. Forman?" Mildred asked.

"Oh, let's see now. It's ten years already. I was a teacher before."

"I was too," Kulak offered. "A principal, too."

"Oh… I never reached that status. Where? In some small town?" Mr. Forman asked.

"No, right here in Los Angeles," Kulak answered.

"You didn't like teaching?" Mildred asked Mr. Forman.

"I got tired of the kids. And the parents were even worse. The money wasn't enough, either."

"Yes, that's for certain," Mr. Kulak, said.

"This job pays better?" Mildred asked.

"It certainly does."

"You have children?" Mildred asked.

"Yes, two. My daughter just started college in Massachusetts."

"Harvard?" Stanley asked.

"No Williams College."

"That's a fine school," Mr. Kulak said.

"Yes, it is. But what an expensive one, even with a small scholarship," Forman said.

Stanley sensed Forman's uneasiness and said, "Well, like I said, we corrected everything on the list you left. Why don't I show you?" The three residents smiled proudly as Stanley lead Forman out of the office. Stanley stopped and pointed to the ceiling outside his office, "There's one of the new smoke detectors. We replaced them all over the house." They went out the front door where Stanley pointed to the new cement that he repaired. He and his three residents were proud of the work they had done and smiled.

"That's very good," Mr. Forman said.

"Let me show you the rest of the house," Stanley said.

"That won't be necessary. I'll take your word for it." He reached into his briefcase, pulled out a sheet of paper, and handed it to Stanley. "I'm afraid there are other violations—this is the addendum to the original list."

Stanley looked befuddled and took the paper. Mildred and the others huddled around Stanley, peering at it. "What's this? I have a license."

"The license is in Muriel Cutler's name."

"That's my mother. She passed away two years ago. I've been running the place ever since she was diagnosed with cancer."

"I'm sorry for your loss Mr. Cutler, but you'll have to apply for a license in your own name if you plan to continue operating this business."

Mildred could not contain herself any longer, "This sounds like harassment! Most of the things you have here aren't even true. Trash in the front yard? Where do you see trash in the front yard? Stanley's always cleaning the grounds."

Stanley looked nervous, and said to Mildred, "Shh!" and turned his attention back to Forman. "I'll get these things taken care of."

Mr. Kulak read, "Insufficient trash containers? What kind of bullshit is that?"

"It's plain and simple—harassment. I've seen it before," Mildred said.

Sensing the growing hostility, Mr. Forman shifted nervously. "And I suggest you keep your residents out of our administrative problems." He turned and walked out of the front yard.

"And I suggest..." Mildred started to say, but Stanley put his hand over her mouth. Miss Louise stuck her tongue out at the departing man. Mr. Kulak raised a middle finger in the air, and Stanley immediately grabbed Kulak's hand and covered the offending finger.

CHAPTER 24

That night, the residents sat around the dining room table. Mildred held the list that Forman left. She looked over it and said, "I've seen this before. You correct these things and they will be back with another list. Have they done this before, Stanley?"

"No. Not since I've been here." He looked around the table. They all shook their heads, indicating they had never witnessed it either.

"There's something suspicious going on. We need to go to their offices and protest," Mildred said.

"Mildred, you think it's harassment?" Mr. Benson asked.

"It seems that way to me," Mildred answered.

"I don't know… A protest sounds serious," Stanley said. However, he was no stranger to protests; he had actively protested the Vietnam War, nuclear weapons and joined the civil rights movement.

"This is serious. I don't want to lose another home," Mildred said.

"Mildred's right. Our home is being threatened," Mrs. Benson, pointed out.

"I'm tired of them taking advantage of us old folks. We have rights and we have to stand up for them," Mildred preached.

"It sounds like fun if you ask me," Mrs. Bennetti

said as she twisted the tiles of a Rubik's Cube in her hands.

Stanley looked around the table. "If it's all right with all of you, we'll do it."

"Good. We'll go down there on Monday," a fired-up Mildred said.

They all stopped talking as they stared at Mrs. Bennetti twisting the square of multi-colored tiles.

"What in the world is that thing, Anna?" Mrs. Benson asked.

Without looking up, Mrs. Bennetti said, "It's a Rubik's Cube. I found it on the bus today. I wanted to give it to the driver. He showed me a whole bag of them that people left. He said, 'People get frustrated and just leave them.' You gotta get the same color on all sides."

"Looks pretty complicated to me," Stanley said.

Mildred looked at her watch. "I have to get to services. Stanley, will you come with me?"

It took Stanley by surprise. "Me?"

"Yes. It won't take long. Maybe, we can enlist some supporters at the service. You have something else to wear?"

Stanley looked at his jeans and denim shirt. "I'm not even Jewish."

As Mildred got up from the table, she said, "That's okay. God won't mind. But hurry up! Go change."

Shortly after, Mildred and Stanley came out the front door. She wore a dark gray dress and low black heels. Stanley wore an ill-fitting, slightly wrinkled black suit, and an open-collared white shirt. Walking up the street, he fussed with a dark-colored tie, trying to put it into a knot. "I hope this protest doesn't cause more trouble," he said.

"It won't. I'm gonna say a few prayers tonight that everything goes well."

When they got to the synagogue, people entered the block-long building on Hollywood Boulevard. Inside, Stanley took a seat and Mildred said, "I'm going to ask the rabbi to make an announcement about the protest."

Before Stanley could say anything, Mildred walked up to the rabbi and spoke to him. Stanley gazed around the enormous room. Mildred must have been persuasive because after a few moments, the rabbi was nodding in agreement with Mildred's request.

CHAPTER 25

Monday morning, a protest was in full swing in front of the downtown high-rise office building, housing the licensing commission offices. A surprisingly large crowd of protestors, mostly seniors, recruited by Mildred and the residents of Star Bright, carried signs that read: LEAVE OUR HOME ALONE; STOP HARRASSING SENIORS, MORE SOCIAL SECURITY LESS HARASSMENT; SOCIAL JUSTICE FOR ALL. They marched in a wide circle, chanting: "Leave our home alone! Leave our home alone!"

The Star Bright people marched alongside their sympathizers. Stanley and Mildred were absent from the crowd. They sat on a couch on the seventeenth floor, opposite the reception desk of the licensing commission, waiting for a face-to-face with the commissioner.

They were happy to see employees gathered around the windows watching and discussing the protest down on the plaza. The receptionist, a young woman, wore black-framed glasses; she was overly courteous to Stanley and Mildred when they first arrived, but her initial reaction turned icy when she found out they were responsible for the protest. As she opened mail, she occasionally glanced over at them disdainfully.

Behind the closed office door next to her desk, Mr. Forman and his boss, Licensing Commissioner Mr. Raines, a middle-aged graying man in an expensive-looking suit, also looked out the window at the protestors. "Our plan is to shut the place down. Whatever, that takes," Raines said with a sinister look. "If we can get them to call off this protest before the news media gets a hold of it, we'll leave them alone for awhile. Let things settle down."

Confidently, Mr. Forman said, "They are in violation."

"And we do have the law on our side," Mr. Raines confirmed.

"This woman seems to be the organizer. She's pushy and shrewd. I have someone checking into her background. I suspect she's one of those professional agitators."

"Let me know what you find out. For now, let's meet with them and feel them out."

The buzzer on the receptionist's intercom sounded. Stanley and Mildred looked up. "Yes, Mr. Raines, right away!" She hung up the phone. "He can see you now. Just go in."

Mildred jumped up and headed for the closed door. Stanley lagged behind. Mildred pushed through the door and Stanley followed her into the spacious office. Raines sat behind a dark wood desk and Forman stood next to his boss with his arms folded across his chest.

Mildred strode right up to the desk. "Good morning gentlemen. I'm Mildred Meyers, the organizer of the protest. This is Stanley Cutler, the owner of the house in question." Mildred glanced at Forman. "Your Mr. Forman here is harassing Stanley and threatening to close our home. We want it stopped! This protest will continue until the harassment stops."

Raines leveled a steady gaze at Mildred. "Well, Mrs. Meyers… It is Meyers?"

"Yes, that's my name."

"There are some serious violations at the house. In fact, your owner doesn't even have a license."

"That's being taken care of. And the rest is harassment."

"I don't agree with that statement at all. Our job is to see that people living in small places like yours meet the same standards as larger institutions. I don't see this as harassment but a fact of life. So until the violations are corrected and Mr. Cutler obtains proper licensing, I don't see that we have anything further to discuss."

An astonished looking Mildred barked, "How can you—"

Mr. Raines cut her off and stated coldly, "Thank you very much for stopping in and stating your case, Mrs. Meyers, Mr. Cutler. Good day!"

The man's attitude infuriated Mildred. She said, "Then, we'll be right outside your window if you change your mind, Mr. Raines—just send for us."

As Stanley and Mildred came out the front door, they noticed the crowd had grown exponentially. More people stepped off a city bus parked at the curb and joined the marchers. The crowd chanted: "Leave our home alone!" Mildred and Stanley re-joined them. All the while, two figures continued to watch them from Mr. Raines' office.

CHAPTER 26

That evening after dinner, Stanley wore his khaki work clothes. The cabinet doors under the kitchen sink sat open, its contents spread out on the floor as Stanley worked to fix a leaking pipe. Mrs. Watanabe watched Stanley as she put on her coat and hat. Speaking softly, Mrs. Watanabe said, "She was in here again tonight telling me what to do."

"She just loves to be in the kitchen. Please try to be patient with her. It will get better."

"If this keeps up, I'm leavin'. I'm telling you Stanley. And this stupid sink gave me trouble all day. I couldn't get any hot water."

"Don't worry, I'll have it fixed." She looked doubtfully at him. "Everybody's a little uptight about the protest. Things will calm down once we get these people out of our hair."

Mr. Benson rushed into the kitchen. "Stanley! Stanley, hurry up. The game is starting."

Stanley turned to him. "Okay, I'll be there as soon as I finish here." Mr. Benson quickly dashed out of the kitchen.

Mrs. Watanabe pleaded, "Please finish the sink."

"I will. I promise. It'll be working fine tomorrow. Goodnight!"

"Goodnight!" He watched her go out the door,

picked up a different wrench, and then ducked his head back under the sink.

CHAPTER 27

The men of Star Bright sat in the living room completely absorbed in Monday night football. Ellen O'Connor, Mr. Kulak's youngest daughter, sat next to him. Ellen played basketball and field hockey in high school. She still had an athlete's well-defined body despite her thirty-plus years, and she was very attractive with a full head of black hair.

The women in the house more or less ignored the men's enthusiasm for the game and sat at the other end of the room. Mildred worked on her knitting, Mrs. Benson scribbled on a crossword puzzle, Miss Louise had a volume of the *Complete Works of William Shakespeare* cracked open, and Mrs. Bennetti worked frantically on her Rubik's Cube.

From the other end of the room, Mr. Benson protested, "That's the third time they got to him. They're coming right over center. What's wrong with that center?"

"That's the easiest way to get to him. They'll keep doing it until the Rams figure out how to plug that hole," Stanley said.

"They never could stop a blitz," Kulak added.

"Dad! Dad!" Ellen pulled on her father's arm, until he looked at her. "Dad—I have to go."

"Wait 'til after this play."

Ellen got up slowly with her eyes on the TV.

Mrs. Benson watched Ellen sympathetically. "You'd think they had enough on Sunday," she said to Ellen.

"I read in *Variety* they're going to have Thursday Night football as well," Miss Louise said.

Kulak stood and kissed his daughter on the cheek. "Thank you for coming. See you next time."

"Yes, Dad." Watching her father sit back down, she approached the other women and said, "I don't know why I come see him during football season."

"I know what you mean, dear. They're like the three stooges," Mrs. Benson said out of the side of her mouth.

"We have to find something else to get them interested in," Mildred suggested.

"I hope you find something." Ellen laughed. Noticing Mildred's knitting, she asked, "What are you making?"

"An Afghan for my daughter."

Ellen noticed Mrs. Bennetti fiddling with her cube and said, "Oh, you have a Rubik's Cube, Mrs. Bennetti." Bennetti hardly looked up. "I had one. I gave up on it. It's too frustrating. I gave it to my kids to play with."

"Oh, I know. But I'm gonna get it," Mrs. Bennett said.

"I just don't seem to have the time for anything like that with the kids and all their activities."

"How many children do you have?" Mildred asked.

"Three, Tommy's the youngest, he's five, Mary is eight, and Artie is the oldest. He's going on twelve."

"Once they grow up—you'll have plenty of time to yourself. Believe me," Mrs. Bennetti said.

"Oh, I sure hope so. It was nice to have met you, Mildred."

"Yes—same here."

"Good luck with your protest. Goodnight!"

The women said their goodbyes. Ellen looked back into the room, and was about to say something else to her dad when a touchdown was scored. Ellen decided it was useless and left.

CHAPTER 28

The next day outside the licensing commission, news of the protest had spread, and as a result, the crowd was much larger than the previous day. Members of the press scurried about with video cameras interviewing protestors, adding credibility to the protest. A small ragtime band of seniors provided entertainment. Several old folks danced to the music while others carried signs and chanted.

Upstairs in the commissioner's office, Raines and Forman stood at the window looking down at the crowd. "It's taking on a carnival atmosphere," Mr. Forman said.

"It's all over the news today. We have to put a stop to this immediately. I got a call from the mayor's office," the commissioner said.

They turned away from the window. "Why don't we just leave them alone for a while? We'll find some other means to shut the place down," Forman said.

Mr. Raines contemplated the situation, and then said, "We'll have to. Has the new license been issued yet?"

"I'll check on it."

"Give him his license and let's get them out of here."

CHAPTER 29

A victory celebration was in progress that evening at Star Bright. Stanley opened a bottle of sparkling apple cider. The residents surrounded him in the dining room and cheered when the cork made a loud popping sound. Stanley filled everyone's glass. When he finished, they raised their glasses. "To our victory!" he said.

"To our victory!" they all joined in.

"This is a big victory for senior citizens everywhere," Mr. Benson said.

"I don't think we could have done it without all the support we got from the community," Mildred added.

"The news people were a big help too. They got the word out," Miss Louise said.

"That man in the wheelchair made all those wonderful signs," Mildred said, smiling.

Miss Louise said, "Mark, I know him. He's a stuntman. He was paralyzed by a stunt that went wrong. He's been in that chair more than twenty years."

"Oh, that poor thing," Mrs. Benson said.

"And the people from SCORE were very nice," Mildred said, looking at the Bensons. "I told them about you. We're going to their next meeting." The Bensons looked a little apprehensive.

"What about that band? They were a hoot," Mrs. Bennetti said.

"They reminded me of bands back in Boston in my youth," Mr. Kulak said, and punctuated it with a few dance steps and holding his arms up in a dancing posture.

"You know they play at the Hollywood Senior Center. I invited them to come over Monday night," Mildred said.

Kulak looked surprised. "They're going to play here?" he asked.

"Yes, I asked them and they said they'd love to. They said they usually practice during the week so they'll use it as a practice session."

Stanley seemed uncomfortable with the idea. "Monday night? The game is on…"

Mr. Benson thought for a moment before he said, "That's right. We'll miss the game."

Mildred quickly suggested, "You can miss one game."

The men seemed to consider the possibility. Stanley asked, "Who's playing?" No one seemed to know the answer.

Having a change-of-heart, Stanley said, "I used to play drums. Maybe I could play a little with them."

"I'm sure they'd be happy to have you join them," Mildred said, encouragingly.

Mrs. Benson turned to her husband and said, "Jim! Why don't you play your clarinet?" To the others, "He was very good back in the day."

Mr. Benson raised an eyebrow in recognition. "Sure, you can play, too," Mildred said.

"Tomorrow at Disneyland, senior citizens get in free. What about going to Disneyland to celebrate our victory?" Stanley asked.

Everyone responded enthusiastically. Kulak laughed. "You'll be the only one who has to pay, Stanley."

"Funny. We'll leave right after breakfast. If that's all right with everyone."

They all nodded their approval.

Miss Louise said, "I haven't been in years. I used to know Walt pretty well. I did some voiceover work in some of his early cartoons."

CHAPTER 30

The next morning was warm and sunny, a perfect day for a trip to Disneyland. After breakfast, the residents gathered in front of the house, waiting for Stanley to back the van down the driveway. Mrs. Benson wore a red Hawaiian shirt over white pants with a wide-brimmed straw hat. Her husband also wore a brightly colored Hawaiian shirt over a clashing pair of brown and white plaid trousers, and an old beat up, floppy fishing hat. Both had on white tennis shoes. Mrs. Bennetti dressed in her racetrack garb, a straw Hollywood Park hat, black high-top sneakers, and a white tee shirt with a thoroughbred's head emblazoned on the front, hanging over baggy khaki pants. Miss Louise looked a little overdressed in an expensive-looking white cotton pantsuit, Birkenstock sandals, and a floppy red hat. Mr. Kulak wore his usual black tee shirt, jeans, sneakers and a shiny red Boston Red Sox jacket. Mildred sported a blue and white print cotton dress, not very comfortable low high-heel shoes, and carried a pink cloth shopping bag.

Stanley backed the van down the driveway, stopping in front of the residents. He got out and slid the side door back for them to get in. He had on an old denim jacket with patches, jeans, and a Mickey Mouse tee shirt. "Everybody get in. I'm gonna get a wheelchair."

"What do you mean? We don't need that," Mildred said.

"We might need it if anyone gets tired." Despite their protests, Stanley went into the house and returned pushing a folded wheelchair.

"Why bother with that, Stanley?" Mr. Kulak asked.

Stanley ignored the comment as he opened the rear doors, put the chair in, and closed them. "Come on, everybody, let's get in."

"Stanley, you're treating us like we're old and feeble," Miss Louise complained.

"It's going to be a long day with a lot of walking," Stanley said as he helped them one-by-one into the van.

The van pulled out of the driveway and turned up the street. Mildred said, "I've always wanted to go there. I remember watching on television when they were building it. Nancy wanted me to take her, but she was always so busy with dance lessons and all her extra curriculum activities, we never could find the time to come out here and go."

"Oh, you're going to love it, Mildred," Miss Louise said.

The residents were all aboard the Disneyland parking lot tram as it pulled up to the entrance gates. They disembarked. Stanley pushed the opened wheelchair in front of him as they stepped into the long line of people waiting to buy tickets, many of them also seniors. The line moved quickly, and before they knew it, they were in the park walking down Main Street. Mrs. Bennetti spotted characters dressed in Mickey and Minnie costumes. "Somebody take my picture with Minnie and Mickey," she said. She pulled a small Kodak camera from her bag and held it out. Stanley took the camera. Over the next few minutes, there were different combinations of pictures with the characters. Mrs. Bennetti stood between them, and then Kulak and Mildred posed for a picture, followed by the Bensons. Miss Louise slid between Minnie and Mickey and Stanley snapped a photo.

"Stanley, get in a picture," Mildred urged.

"Give me the camera, Stanley," Mr. Benson said.

They all watched with wide smiles as Stanley stood between the characters with a beaming smile on his face. After the photo, they proceeded down the street and into Adventure Land.

"Let's go on the jungle ride," Mrs. Benson said. Stanley parked the wheelchair alongside the strollers and carriages at the entrance to the line. The line was long, but it moved quickly.

When they got off the ride, Stanley retrieved the wheelchair and they started to walk. Miss Louise looked at the empty chair Stanley was pushing. "Well if you're going to push that damn thing all over the park, let me get in," she said.

Stanley looked pleased as she sat in the chair. When they got to Space Mountain, there was some debate over who would go on the ride and who would not. Finally, they all decided to go. A young female Disney associate noticed them and Miss Louise sitting in the chair, and signaled them to get out of line and follow her. "Since you have someone in a wheelchair, you don't have to wait in line. We'll move you up to the front." Miss Louise was about to say something but held her tongue. Stanley pushed the chair forward until they were at the front of the line. Stanley helped Miss Louise out of the chair. She did a little acting bit to make it look like she had a mobility problem and got into one of the cars that just pulled in. The others followed in the next few cars, and they zoomed away into the darkness.

When they got off the ride, the men looked fine, but the women were white with fright. "I would never have gone if I knew it was a roller coaster," Mildred said. "I've always hated roller coasters."

Mrs. Benson looked sternly at Stanley, and said, "And in the dark, no less."

Mrs. Bennetti, still shaken, said, "I thought it was fun."

"So why are you so pale?" Miss Louise asked.

"I didn't say I wasn't scared." They all laughed.

For the rest of the day, everyone took turns in the wheelchair and the group didn't have to wait on line.

They stayed late into the night in order to watch the Main Street Electrical Parade and fireworks. It was well after midnight when they got back into the van with exhausted-looking faces. Stanley felt as tired as his residents did. Heads started to drop shortly after the van left the parking lot. "Well, that was sure a fun day," Mr. Kulak said. Mrs. Benson was already half asleep, her head resting on her husband's shoulder, who had also dozed off. Mrs. Bennetti was out cold. Miss Louise rested her head on her hand, which was propped on the armrest at her side.

Kulak soon fell asleep. Mildred sat next to him and her head bobbed up and down as she teetered between consciousness and sleep. Finally, her head dropped to one side and rested on Mr. Kulak's shoulder. Kulak's eyes opened, he looked at Mildred, then put his arm around her shoulders and went back to sleep.

Stanley had to wake everyone after pulling into the Star Bright driveway. "I'm sleeping here," a semi-conscience Kulak, said.

"No, you're not," Mildred said.

Stanley helped everyone out of the vehicle. They stood behind him as he opened the front door, turned on the lights, and stooped over to pick up the day's mail from the floor. The weary residents made their way slowly into the house. Stanley sorted through the mail and gave pieces to the appropriate resident. He stared at one envelope in particular. A troubled look crossed his face as he opened it and scanned the letter. "Oh, no," he said.

The others stopped halfway up the stairs. "What's the matter?" Mildred asked.

"Bad news. It's from the IRS. They're auditing me."

"Have you been paying your taxes?"

"Yes. It says I can't have a business that loses money more than five years. They consider it a hobby. Believe me, this isn't a hobby." He looked devastated. "They want me to bring all my records for the last five years. That's a problem—the books are a mess. And I can't make heads or tails out of my mother's accounting."

"Don't worry I'll help you get them straightened out." Stanley looked doubtful. Mildred attempted to assure him. "I was a bookkeeper. I know how to handle these things."

"There you are Stanley. Get a good night's sleep and you two can tackle this in the morning," Mr. Benson offered.

Everyone said goodnight and went off to their respective rooms.

CHAPTER 31

After breakfast the next morning, Mildred and Stanley huddled in his office with accounting ledgers piled on the desk in front of them. Calculator tapes hung over the front of his desk onto the floor. Mildred carefully scanned the ledger pages and took notes on a yellow pad. Stanley nervously watched her. "You were right. These are a mess," she said.

"Can you fix them?"

"We'll see."

"We don't have a lot of time. Do you have to take so many notes?"

"Stop getting nervous. I'm supposed to be the nervous one. Where are your checkbooks?"

Stanley went to the file cabinet, removed a file containing checkbooks, and handed it to Mildred. She looked at the various check registers and selected one in particular. She leafed through the pages, comparing them to entries in the ledger before her. "Where's the current balance?"

Apologetically, Stanley said, "I haven't been able to balance it for the last six months."

"Stanley, how can you go without balancing your checkbook?"

"I'm not very good at business stuff. Science was my thing."

"Even scientists balance their checkbooks," she scolded. "Where are your cancelled checks?"

Stanley went to the file cabinet again and took out another folder with cancelled checks hanging out. He handed it to Mildred. She looked at the folder disparagingly. "These aren't in any kind of order." She frowned and began sorting the checks. "You have to take care of your books every day. That's how to run a successful business. You need to attend the SCORE meeting with Pauline and Jim to learn some best practices."

CHAPTER 32

Several days later, Mildred, Stanley, and the Benson's attended a SCORE meeting at an office building on Wilshire Boulevard. There were several younger people with older business people mentoring the young folks. They all sat around a large conference table and spoke in hushed tones. "I was just telling Stanley the other day that I always took care of my books at the end of the day," Mildred said.

A young executive wearing glasses with thick lenses answered, "I never seem to have time at the end of the day, nor the energy to tackle the task. I usually wind up coming in on the weekends to catch up."

Stanley chimed in, "I'm with you man."

"You have to make the time," Mildred said. "You let it pile up and it takes even longer. It will make your work at the end of the month easier. And especially at tax time—it will make a big difference." She looked around the table at the young men and women, and they nodded in agreement.

Mr. Benson nodded as well. He said, "Accurate bookkeeping means a lot when you have to go to a bank for money. You have to present them a positive image. Don't be afraid to show them a lot of facts and figures."

"Once they know you, you don't have to do as much to get them on your side," Mrs. Benson said.

"You have to remember—banks are conservative. They won't lend you their money if they are uncertain about the risk involved with lending to you," Mr. Benson emphasized.

When they returned home, the Bensons and Stanley looked as though the SCORE meeting had been worthwhile.

"If you want me to help out with the bookkeeping, Mildred, I would be happy to lend my efforts," Mr. Benson said.

"Thank you, Jim, but I think we have a handle on it," Mildred said. Stanley looked doubtful.

CHAPTER 33

Later that night, the house was dark except for the light streaming out of Stanley's office. Mildred and Stanley sat at the desk. They looked weary as they leaned over ledgers and sorted receipts. Stanley sipped from a can of Coke. Mildred picked up an invoice. "This is what you pay the cook?" she asked. At that hour of night, all Stanley could do was to muster a nod.

"It's too much. She's so unreasonable. Today, I told her about my cooking class tomorrow. She got so annoyed. She started slamming cabinet doors." Stanley looked sympathetic. "I wish you'd just get rid of her."

"I can't. Good cooks are hard to find."

"I'll do the cooking!"

"I can't have you doing the cleaning and the cooking, too."

"Everyone could help. It would be fun. It'll give them something else to do."

Stanley shook his head in disagreement. He rubbed his eyes and looked at his digital watch. "It's late. We better quit."

Mildred looked at the mess on the desk. "We didn't make much of a dent."

"Yeah. We'll work on it tomorrow. Let's get to bed."

He turned the desk light off. They both got up. “Think about it. Get rid of her.”

“Mrs. Meyers, I don’t think I can do that. Goodnight!

“Goodnight, Stanley.”

CHAPTER 34

All the residents, plus Stanley, stood around the center counter in the kitchen. Everyone seemed to be enjoying themselves except Mrs. Watanabe, who stood off to the side with a displeased look on her face. The table had flour all over it, cartons of eggs, pots and pie pans. Mildred stood in the middle of the group; the front of her dress covered in white flour.

Mr. Kulak looked at the table and around the room. "Where's the cheese? Did somebody cut the cheese," he laughed at his own joke.

Miss Louise lifted a large piece of cheddar. "Here," she said. They passed the cheese to him. He took it and grated it.

Mildred watched him. "That looks like enough, Arthur. Now add it to your egg mixture." Kulak scooped it up and dumped it into the mixer bowl. Mrs. Benson turned on the mixer. "Not too fast," Mildred advised. She peeked at the swirling mixture and said, "That should be good. Now, let's put it into the pie shells."

Mrs. Benson turned off the machine, removed the bowl, and filled her pie pan with the gooey mixture. She gave the bowl to Miss Louise who looked at the filling. "It's not too liquidy?" she asked.

"No, it's just right. It will tighten up in the oven," Mildred said.

One by one, they each filled their pie pans. Mildred said, "Now, we put them in the oven."

Mrs. Bennetti was closest to the oven so she opened the door. They handed their pans to her. She put them carefully on the oven shelves and closed the door.

"They need to bake forty- to fifty-minutes," Mildred said.

Mrs. Watanabe glared at them from where she sat across the room cutting up vegetables. While the residents stood around chatting, Mr. Kulak left the kitchen.

Forty-minutes later, Mildred opened the oven door. "You just stick a knife in the center to see if it comes out clean." She tested one of the quiche. "It looks good." She removed it from the oven and put it on the table. "We have to let it stand five minutes. This one is yours, Stanley."

Stanley looked proudly at his quiche. "It looks delicious." They all admired it.

Mildred pulled out another one. "And I think this is Arthur's." She put it on the table and looked around for Kulak, but he wasn't there. She went back to the oven tested one, and pulled it out. "I think this is yours Anna.

"Oh, how nice," Mrs. Bennetti said.

Mildred removed another quiche and placed it on the table. "Louise I think this is yours."

Miss Louise didn't see it because she was looking toward the door. "Oh no!" she shrieked.

"No, it looks good Louise," Mildred insisted.

"Arthur!" Miss Louise said.

The rest of them turned in the direction she was

looking, only to see Kulak bent over with his back to them, his pants around his thighs, and his rear end exposed. "Arthur! That's a disgusting thing to do in the kitchen," Miss Louise said.

Mildred almost dropped the last pie. Noticing, Mrs. Benson said, "Be careful, Mildred. I told you he's a pervert."

Mildred looked shocked. Kulak pulled up his pants and quickly exited through the door. Stanley followed him, yelling, "Mr. Kulak! Mr. Kulak wait! I want to talk to you."

"Mrs. Bennetti said, "Did you see that scrotum? It's almost to his knees. It's just like us." She cupped her breasts and made a downward swooping motion with her hands, "Everything just drops."

CHAPTER 35

From the looks of the empty plates on the dining room table, and the satisfied faces on everyone, the quiche was a success. Mr. Kulak was very quiet during dinner. The others tried engaging him in conversation but they could not draw him out. His face reflected his guilty conscience about the earlier incident.

Mildred popped up from her seat and started clearing the table. "I'm going to the senior citizens center this week. I want all of you to come," she looked around the table and only received a few raised eyebrows. She turned her attention towards Kulak. "Arthur!" He looked surprised when he heard his name. "You and I are going to talk to the director about having you teach some history classes."

"I don't know about that, Mildred. It's been years since I've done any teaching. And my memory is getting bad."

"Oh, you don't forget how to do something like that."

"I think you would do a wonderful job, Arthur." Miss Louise commented. For Mildred's benefit, she said, "He has such a wonderful knowledge of the subject."

Mildred was about to carry a pile of dishes into the kitchen. "And Louise you'll love some of the arts and crafts they're doing."

"I don't know if I want to participate. Besides, I'm waiting for an important call from my agent this week," Miss Louise said.

"Oh, you'll love it," Mildred said over her shoulder as she went into the kitchen; the others got up and left the dining room.

Mrs. Watanabe made a face and went to the other side of the room when she saw Mildred enter the kitchen. Mildred took out plastic wrap and wrapped the leftover quiche in small packages. On the other side of the room, Mrs. Watanabe was opening and closing cabinets. Finally, she asked, "Have you seen that big orange bowl?"

"I used it to put the fruit salad in."

"I wish you would leave things alone in here. I can't find anything in this kitchen since you've been here." She slammed the cabinet door and stared at Mildred with contempt.

"The way you do things, it's amazing you find anything. This place can use a good reorganization."

"This is my kitchen and I put things where I can easily find them." Her voice rose a few octaves and she said, "I'm getting sick and tired of hearing how you do everything right and I do everything wrong."

"Don't you yell at me," Mildred shouted back.

"You know, my family was put in an internment camp during the war. That's where I grew up. So I'm not taking any guff from you. I don't need this aggravation or this job!" She picked a dish off the counter and smashed it on the floor, then left the kitchen. Mildred, in shock, watched her leave. The crash brought the Bensons into the room.

Meanwhile, Mrs. Watanabe charged into Stanley's office. He looked up and said, "What's going on back there?"

Mrs. Watanabe tore off her apron and threw it on Stanley's desk. "I told you, Stanley, it's either me or that woman. I quit!"

"Wait! Please Mrs. Watanabe. Don't go."

She stormed out of the room, leaving a confused and helpless looking Stanley.

CHAPTER 36

Following Mrs. Watanabe's hasty departure, Stanley sat in his office behind his desk. Mr. Kulak, with a guilty looking face, sat on the office bench. Stanley shook his head, "Can this day get any worse?"

"Some days are like that," Kulak said.

"What's going on with you?

"What do you mean?"

"You know what I mean. You dropping your pants and mooning everyone."

Kulak shifted uncomfortably and said, "Stanley, I was just having a little fun. Everyone seemed so serious. I just wanted to add a little levity."

"That's not a proper thing to do."

"I don't see the problem with a little nudity."

"The others don't like you doing things like that."

"I've been a naturist most of my adult life. Do you know that Benjamin Franklin was fond of being naked, and John Quincy Adams, too? I hear your President Kennedy was a nudist too."

"I'm sure they didn't go around shocking people like you do. And don't start with me about President Kennedy."

Mr. Kulak looked mildly concerned.

"I personally don't have a problem with nudity, but there is a proper place and time for it. Myself, I was a member of a commune and didn't wear clothes for days at a time."

"Well see. You understand then."

"I want you to promise to stop doing that. And please wear your robe or pajamas to the bathroom during the night."

Kulak looked frustrated. "Stanley, I won't promise anything, but I'll try to contain my desires to parade around in the buff."

"Please don't try. Just don't do it anymore. I appreciate your cooperation, Mr. Kulak."

"Now, if you are through chastising me, I'd like to go to my room."

"Oh, sure. Goodnight! Please close the door on your way out."

Kulak stood up and bowed slightly to Stanley, went out the door, and closed it behind him. Stanley heaved a big sigh, leaned back in his chair, opened his desk drawer, and pulled out a plastic bag with marijuana. He rolled a joint, lit it, and inhaled the smoke. A familiar mellow feeling came over him.

CHAPTER 37

The Downtown Los Angeles Produce Market was alive with activity as Stanley and Mildred entered the facility. Workers and customers pushed hand trucks with produce hanging over the sides of boxes. Outside, cars and trucks snarled the streets surrounding the market. Stanley followed Mildred. With an eagle eye for bargains, Mildred scanned the various vendor's stalls and counters overflowing with colorful fruits and vegetable. "I'm going to call her later and see if she'll come back," Stanley said.

Mildred stopped. "She's crazy. She got like a maniac with me."

"I asked you to please try to get along with her."

"It wasn't me. We're better off without her."

Stanley shook his head in disagreement. He followed Mildred over to a counter with a pile of fresh, green lettuce. Customers were buying it as well as other produce; produce workers at the stand helped with purchases. One of the produce men, a middle-aged guy with a potbelly and wearing a L.A. Dodger's baseball cap, walked up to Mildred and Stanley, and asked, "Can I help you madam?"

"How much is your lettuce?"

"Fifteen-cents a head."

Mildred's surprised look put him on the defensive.

He said, "What?"

Mildred said to Stanley, "Come on, they're selling them for twelve-cents at the other end."

Stanley looked embarrassed because they hadn't been to the other end of the market, yet. Mildred started to walk away.

"Stanley, come on, these guys are crooks."

"Hey, come on lady, give me a break," the produce man pleaded.

Mildred grabbed Stanley's arm and before they even took two steps, the man stopped them. "How many you want, lady?"

"Six. But not at these prices."

"Lady, for you, twelve cents a head. How's that sound?"

Mildred stopped walking and turned around. "That's better. And don't give me the old stuff."

The man smiled at Stanley. "You got a tough mother there."

"He's not my son," Mildred said.

The man shrugged his shoulders and gave Stanley an I-didn't-know look.

With an eye for value and freshness, Mildred inspected some of the other vegetables and fruits while the man watched her. "Where are these onions from?"

"Fresno. You want some? For you ten-cents a pound." Mildred looked a little bit astonished.

"Give me five pounds." She took one out of his hand. "I don't want any bruised ones, either." She put it down and replaced it with a better-looking onion.

"Where you from lady, New York?"

"How did you know?"

"Your accent. Ah, I'm from New York, too. I

couldn't stand it when the Dodgers left Brooklyn so I moved my family out here. You got a good eye for produce."

"I should. I worked in the market until I was sixty-five." Stanley paced nervously behind them.

"Yeah? Who'd you work for?"

"Sambucci. I worked for Angelo Sambucci."

"Jeez, my brother-in-law's place is right next door."

"Tony Garelli's? I used to change his diapers when he was a baby. Big Tony was a good friend of mine. He was always trying to get me to work for him. God bless his soul."

"What'd ya do at Sambucci's?"

"Bookeeping."

"She's good. She's helping me get my books straight," Stanley said.

"Wait till I tell my wife. So what—are you livin' out here now?" All the while, he continued to fill a bag with a variety of fruit.

"Yes, my daughter lives here. But she doesn't have room for me, so I'm living in Stanley's house."

The vendor looked at Stanley and extended his hand. "Johnny Mancini."

Stanley shook his hand and said, "Stanley Cutler."

"Hey, nice to meet ya." He asked Mildred, "And what's your name?"

"Mildred Meyers." He took her hand in his and patted the back of it.

"Always nice to meet a fellow New Yorker, Mildred. Whatta ya Jewish?"

"Yeah."

"Jews, Italians, we're all the same. Am I right?" Mildred nodded in agreement.

"So how much for all this?"

He looked at the bags he filled and said, "For you…" he whispered, "Give me three bucks."

Mildred smiled and counted out three singles. Stanley did a double take.

"You here every day?" Mildred asked.

"Oh, yeah. What else am I gonna do?"

"You got good prices, Johnny. We'll be back again."

As they walked away, Mildred turned to Stanley, and said, "I can't believe that woman did all your shopping at the supermarket. See how much money you're saving already."

Stanley didn't look convinced.

CHAPTER 38

In the evening, everyone sat at the dining room table except Mildred, who was cooking in the kitchen. “Stay away from the door—I’m coming through with a hot dish,” she said. The door to the dining room opened and Mildred walked in with a smoking brisket, steaming on a platter.

“Is there anything we can help with Mildred?” Mrs. Benson asked.

“I just have two more dishes. Somebody, please cut that up,” Mildred said.

“I don’t think we’ve ever had brisket,” Mr. Kulak said. “I love a good brisket.” He picked up the carving knife and fork and began slicing the meat.

“It looks delicious,” Mr. Benson said.

Mildred walked out and quickly returned with a plate piled with hot biscuits and a dish full of vegetables. She put them down and was about to go back into the kitchen.

Stanley stood up and said, “Let me help you.”

“Sit down! Sit down!” Mildred said.

Stanley hesitantly sat back down.

“Ooo, the biscuits look marvelous,” Miss Louise cooed.

“She made them from scratch. I watched her,” Mrs. Bennetti said.

Mildred came out with a bowl of mashed potatoes and a gravy boat. She said, “Don’t wait for me. Start!”

Stanley pleaded, “Come on, Mrs. Meyers, you sit down too.”

“Yes, sit down and eat, Mildred,” Mrs. Bennetti said.

Mildred was about to sit, then hesitated. “I think I left the gas on.”

Stanley stood and said, “Sit, Mrs. Meyers. I’ll go.” He returned a moment later. “No gas on,” and he sat.

As plates passed around, Mildred watched Stanley put a small piece of brisket on his plate. She said to Stanley, “That’s all you’re taking?” She added a larger piece of meat to his plate.

“That’s too big,” Stanley complained.

“You’re a growing boy,” Mr. Kulak said and laughed.

“You’re too skinny. That’s why you’re not married,” Mildred accused. She continued to fill his dish with potatoes, biscuits, and vegetables.

When the plates came around to Mildred’s side of the table, Mrs. Benson said, “Anna, fix her plate.” Mrs. Bennetti filled Mildred’s dish. She placed it in front of Mildred, and Mildred put some of the meat back.

“This is too much. I don’t want all that.”

“You see… You tell me to eat more and look what you’re eating,” Stanley said.

“It’s all right—I was married already.” She surprised everyone and said, “It wasn’t what it was cracked up to be.”

“Oh, see and you want me to marry...”

“With the right person, you wouldn’t regret it, Stanley,” Mr. Kulak said.

"That's absolutely right," Mr. Benson confirmed. He smiled at his wife, who returned the smile, and squeezed her husband's hand affectionately.

"Well, mine wasn't the right person. He left as soon as our daughter was born. Took all our money, too."

"That's terrible, Mildred. What did you do?" Miss Louise asked.

"What can you do? You do the best you can and just start all over again. My sister had two of her own children so she took care of Nancy, and I went back to work."

A silence fell over the room as they all dug into their food. Finally, Mr. Kulak said, "Mildred! Everything is delicious."

"So, Stanley, is Sue coming back?" Mr. Benson asked.

"I left her a message to call me."

Mildred wouldn't look up and pretended not to hear.

"Well, I have to say, Mildred's cooking is a step up," Mr. Benson said. The others agreed with him. No one looked up from their dish as they shoveled food into their mouths.

Mildred turned to Mrs. Bennetti. "I don't want to tell you what to do, but you should stay away from the race track. How much money did you lose this week?"

A little put off by the inquiry, Mrs. Bennetti said, "That's my business."

Coming to her defense, Miss Louise said, "That's her enjoyment."

"It's not right throwing away money like that."

"You enjoy the things you like. I enjoy gambling."

"I stopped at the senior center. You should try it someday. That's where we should all spend our afternoons, and get away from that TV."

The others didn't seem terribly interested except for Kulak, who said, "Mildred, I've been reviewing some of my notes and books and I would be up for a discussion about the causes of the Great Depression."

"Well see that's good," Mildred said.

"I'll work on preparing something. Stanley, perhaps I can use the typewriter in the office?"

"Sure. But you'll have to wait till we finish the books."

"And how is that coming along," Mr. Benson asked.

Mildred answered, "We're getting pretty close to making sense out of them."

CHAPTER 39

Late Sunday morning, Mildred worked in the backyard garden. The Bensons entered the yard. Mr. Benson wore a light blue seersucker suit, white shirt, stripped tie, and a straw fedora on his head. Mrs. Benson had on a pink dress and a pink wide-brimmed hat. Mildred bent over a row of turned up soil and placed seeds.

Oh, you got a lot accomplished," Mrs. Benson said.

Mildred looked up. "Yes, it's going well. How was church?"

"Too long," Mr. Benson said.

"Oh, he's a pain in the neck. I don't listen to him anymore," Mrs. Benson said.

"I don't like when they take too long, either," Mildred said.

Mrs. Bennetti came out the kitchen door followed by her son, Robert, a good-looking man with dark hair in his mid-thirties, and her young grandchildren, Michael and Anna. They walked over and joined Mildred and the Bensons.

Hello. How are you Bob?" Mr. Benson said.

"Fine."

"Hello, Pauline."

"Hello, Robert," Mrs. Benson said. She smiled at the children and said, "They're getting big." Robert smiled with pride.

The Bensons shook hands with Robert.

"Mildred, I want you to meet my family," Mrs. Bennetti said.

Mildred put down her hand shovel and cleaned her hands on her apron.

"This is my son Robert, and Michael and Anna."

"Nice to meet you," Mildred said. "And you have beautiful children." The kids bowed their heads shyly. Mildred shook the man's hand.

"My mother said you're from New York, too."

"Yes."

"How do you like it here?"

"I'm getting used to it. I love the weather. I couldn't take the cold back there anymore." Mildred turned to the children and said to the little girl, "What pretty hair you have. How old are you?" The little girl scrunched up her face, and then, held up three fingers and smiled. To the boy, she asked, "And how old are you?"

"Five," he said in a shy voice.

"Are you taking Grandma home with you today?"

The little boy said, "Yeah."

Mildred said, to Robert, "They're cute."

Mrs. Bennetti looked at her son and said, "Mildred's trying to reform me."

"Good luck! My father was worse."

Mrs. Bennetti quickly answered, "Nev'a mind. Your father was a good man. He liked his gambling, but we always had a roof over our head and plenty of food on the table."

No one responded. They just looked at one another.

"We better get going," Mrs. Bennetti said.

"Nice meeting you. Good luck with your garden."

"Thanks."

"What are you planting?"

"Some herbs for cooking, tomatoes, onions, potatoes…"

"That sounds nice. There's nothing like fresh vegetables," Robert said.

Mildred smiled. To Mrs. Bennetti, Mildred said, "Enjoy yourself."

"Thanks. Let's go."

The Bensons said goodbye and Mrs. Bennetti and her family turned and left. Mr. Benson looked at his watch. "It's almost time for the game." He turned towards the house.

"I better change," Mrs. Benson said. She followed her husband into the house. Mildred went back to work on her garden.

CHAPTER 40

All the lights were out in Star Bright except for the ones burning in Stanley's office; Mildred and Stanley sat at his desk with ledgers still piled on the desk. They both looked tired. Stanley read from an opened ledger in front of him, "Twenty-dollars, one-hundred-fifty, one-hundred twenty-five…" He scanned the rest of the page and said, "That's it."

Mildred rang up the total on the calculator, made an entry in the ledger, and closed it. "We're through with this one," she said. Stanley was pleased but too tired to show it as he placed the ledger on the floor behind him.

Mildred sat back with a pained expression on her face and belched. "Oh, excuse me." She burped again even louder than the first time. A series of loud and not so loud eruptions followed. Each time she said, "Excuse me! But my stomach…"

"Let me get you an Alka-Seltzer." Stanley popped out of his chair and left the room. Mildred removed her glasses, stretched her arms straight out, rubbed the bridge of her nose, yawned, and belched again. Stanley returned with a glass of water. He sat down and dropped two tablets into the glass. They immediately started to sizzle. A concerned look came over his face.

"You must be tired. With all the cooking, cleaning, shopping, and these books."

"Oh, it's nothing."

"Nothing to you but I appreciate all you've done."

Stanley picked up the glass and handed it to Mildred. "Here, drink this!"

Mildred drank the sizzling mixture in one long swallow and made a face. "I won't be able to sleep anyway. Not with this stomach." As she put the empty glass down another rather loud burp came out of her. A relieved look spread across her face.

"Thanks for all your help with this and everything else you've been doing. I don't think I would have been able to do it—straightening these books out." He squeezed her hand in appreciation and Mildred burped again. They both laugh.

"Excuse me, again." Mildred seemed to think of something and burst out laughing.

"What's so funny?"

"I was just thinking about something my father used to say. He said, 'A burp is an unprocessed fart.'"

Stanley smiled. They both fell silent.

"I'm nervous about this audit," Stanley said.

"Don't be." Mildred smiled confidently.

"If I have to pay them anything, I'm in trouble. You know how much I have in the bank."

"I'm telling you—you won't have to pay. We're filing these amended returns. It will show that you made profits two out of the last five years and they owe you money."

"I sure hope you're right. Anything having to do with the government makes me uncomfortable."

Mildred opened her mouth and a series of

reverberating belches came out. They both looked surprised. “Oh, that feels better.” A pleasant smile came over her face and she said, “Maybe, I’ll be able to sleep after all.”

“Good. Let’s call it a night and get to bed.” He switched off the desk lamp and they both got up.

CHAPTER 41

The Bensons sat on the front porch. Mr. Benson read the newspaper while his wife, sitting next to him, worked on a crossword puzzle. Out on the street, a long black limousine stopped in front of the house. Mr. Benson looked up from his paper, noticing the vehicle. The back window cracked open a bit. Someone inside was looking at the house. Mrs. Benson turned her attention to the idling car.

"I wonder if they're lost," Mr. Benson said to his wife, "I better go see if they need help."

He got up, stepped off the porch, and began walking towards the car. Before he reached it, the window zipped shut and the car sped away. Mr. Benson stood there watching, trying to figure out what was going on. Finally, he turned back to the porch where Mrs. Benson looked on.

"What was that all about?" she asked.

"I don't know." He winked at his wife and said, "How about that nap?" She smiled mischievously. She got up and they went through the front door, stopping in the doorway of Stanley's office where Mildred and Stanley were still reconciling the books. Mildred and Stanley looked up.

"Stanley, I don't know what to make of this," Mr. Benson said.

Stanley looked a little puzzled. “What?”

“Well we were sitting on the porch and a big limousine pulled up and stopped. Someone in the back opened the window a little and was looking at the house.”

“Hmm…” Stanley sighed.

“I started over to the car, you know, thinking that they were lost and needed some directions. Just as I got to it, the window closed and they drove off. What do you suppose they wanted?”

Stanley looked at Mildred who gave him a confused look. “It’s probably nothing.” Stanley said.

“I just thought you should know.”

“Yes, thanks.”

“We’re going up to take a nap.”

“Okay. Have a good one.” Stanley smiled knowingly.

The Bensons left. Mildred and Stanley turned their attention back to their work. Moments later, Mrs. Bennetti stood in the doorway with a big smile on her face. She held her cube in her hands and turned the tiles while she smiled and said, “Those two are going up to do it.”

Mildred’s eyes opened wide; Stanley’s face turned beet red. “I wish you wouldn’t say those things,” Stanley said.

“Are you talking about what I think you are talking about?” Mildred asked.

Mrs. Bennetti winked at her. “I sure am.”

“Oh…”

“I say good for them,” Bennetti said.

"She better watch out she doesn't get pregnant," Mildred said, and then laughed at her own joke. Mrs. Bennetti laughed too.

"I just wanted to let you know I won't be home for dinner. I'm going to Gardena to play cards."

"Cards?" Mildred said.

"Poker."

Mildred raised a scornful eyebrow and asked, "I thought you were broke?"

"My son gave me fifty-dollars yesterday."

"The band's coming tonight," Mildred said.

"Oh, I'll be back by then."

"You're going there by bus?" Stanley asked.

"No. My cousin is picking me up. I better get going. Wish me luck."

"I'm not wishing you luck. Leave some money home," Mildred said.

Mrs. Bennetti laughed. "Mildred, I always win at poker."

"Well, I hope you do," Mildred said.

Stanley watched Mrs. Bennetti's fingers manipulating the cube and asked, "How's that going?"

"I'm gonna get this damn thing if it kills me."

Stanley laughed. "Did Mr. Kulak tell you the odds are one in eighteen to the eighteenth power?"

"I don't know what that means, but it sounds like my kind of odds." Outside, a car horn honked. Mrs. Bennetti said, "I'll see you tonight." Mildred and Stanley waved goodbye. Mrs. Bennetti left while Mildred and Stanley went back to work.

It wasn't long before Miss Louise stepped into the office. "Stanley, you better do something right away." She immediately got Stanley's attention.

"What's the matter?

"It's Arthur."

Stanley looked even more attentive.

"I went out to the yard to sit and read and he's sunning himself *AU NATURAL*. And the neighbors are complaining they're going to call the authorities."

Stanley jumped up. "I better go get him."

He walked out of the office and Miss Louise followed him out to the backyard where Kulak was stretch out on a chaise lounge completely naked. "Mr. Kulak!" Stanley shouted.

Kulak eyes opened.

"You can't sit out here naked."

A female neighbor yelled from an upstairs window, "I'm gonna call the cops if that old man doesn't put his clothes on."

"Please don't. He's covering up," Stanley said, apologetically.

"Why not? It's private property," Mr. Kulak said.

"Because this isn't a nudist colony and the neighbors are going to call the cops."

Kulak sighed. "Nosey neighbor. Oh, well, alright." He reached over, picked his robe off the ground, and put it on.

All the while, Stanley watched him carefully. "Thank you."

Kulak smiled at Miss Louise as Stanley went back in the house. "You had to rat me out?"

"Personally, I rather see you nude then in jail."

"Thanks for the compliment."

CHAPTER 42

As Mildred had promised, the ragtime band was in the living room playing. Mr. Sleight, a tall, thin man in his seventies, conducted the band with an easy, relaxed manner. There was also a heavy-set senior keyboard player who sat and played the upright piano. Another elderly man wearing an old-fashioned straw hat with a red band around it played the saxophone. The big surprise was Stanley rhythmically pounding the drums and Jim Benson playing the clarinet. Everyone in the house enjoyed the entertainment.

Mr. Kulak and Miss Louise danced to the swinging music. After a few minutes, it was obvious that Kulak was quite the dancer. Miss Louise was an equally adept partner as Kulak spun her around. The music ended and Miss Louise collapsed into a chair. Kulak looked towards Mildred and said, "Mildred, come on!" He extended a hand towards her.

"Not me," Mildred begged off.

Kulak turned his attention to Mrs. Benson as they began to play another tune. "Pauline!" Mrs. Benson jumped up, and she and Kulak began to dance slowly to the music. The beat picked up and soon they were swirling around the room. Mildred felt a sense of accomplishment in getting the band there. As she tapped her foot to the music, she was delighted everyone was having a good time. Mrs. Bennetti got on her feet and started to shake her full frame provocatively, dancing in front of the band. Mr. Sleight watched her for a few seconds, then stopped conducting the band and started to dance with Bennetti.

The band played until ten o'clock and during the evening, Kulak was the life of the party, dancing with one woman after the other. He even managed to get Mildred up on the floor for a few turns.

CHAPTER 43

Several days later, Mildred and Stanley were downtown Los Angeles approaching the large building housing the IRS offices. At the big glass front door, Mildred opened it, and then turned to look for Stanley, several steps behind. She had to prod him through the door and into the building's lobby, where men and woman in business clothes scurried on and off elevators. They took the elevator to the tenth floor, where a woman directed them to an IRS auditor's desk; the name on his desk read: MR. CLARK. He looked like a befuddled looking middle-aged man with thick glasses. The office was alive with activity; rows of desks went on endlessly, calculator keys clattered, and bits and pieces of conversation floated through the air.

Mildred and Stanley sat in front of the auditor's desk. Mildred opened a ledger, placed it along with receipts and tax forms on the desk in a very organized fashion. "You'll see that there was an operating loss of six-hundred dollars last year," Mildred said.

The auditor looked at the open ledger, the receipts, and tax forms. As he looked up, Mildred handed him a strip of calculator tape and said, "Operating loss six-hundred… Total income," she pointed to an entry on one of the tax forms, "Right there. Then, we took the capital depreciation allowance, and I subtracted fifty-percent of line twenty-seven from line twenty-five, and, as you can see, you owe Stanley one-hundred-five dollars." Stanley cringed a little when Mildred mentioned his name.

Mr. Clark added the figures again on his calculator. Mildred smiled at a tense and worried-looking Stanley; he forced a weak smile. "Your figures are correct Mrs. Meyers," Mr. Clark said.

Stanley appeared relieved for the first time.

"As for the four previous years, here are amended returns." She handed over the completed forms. "Two of those years were profitable with no additional payments due the IRS."

The man took time reviewing each one. Mildred sat confidently, her purse across her lap. Stanley still looked uncomfortable. He squirmed in his seat, perspired, and took off his glasses several times to wipe his brow.

"Let me know if you need an explanation for anything," Mildred said.

Mr. Clark stopped tapping on his calculator and looked up, shaking his head before going back to his calculator. Mildred turned to Stanley and winked, but he was too scared to react.

Mr. Clark finished scrutinizing the last amended return and looked up. "As far as I can see, Mrs. Meyers, your figures are absolutely correct. Is this the address to send the return?"

"Yes, it is." Mildred didn't waste time picking up the ledgers and the rest of their materials.

"If we had more people like you coming in here, it would make my job a lot easier."

"It was nothing. Well, thank you," Mildred said.

She stood, looked over at a petrified Stanley, then pulled him up by the, arm and handed him the ledgers. Stanley half-smiled at the auditor.

As they turned to walk away, Mr. Clark called after them, "Mrs. Meyers!" Mildred stopped and turned around; Stanley kept walking, happy that it was all over. "Would you like a job?" Mr. Clark asked. Mildred looked surprised. "We can use someone like you."

"Thank you. I'm flattered, but I'm retired."

"How about part time?

"Thank you again, but no thanks"

"Just thought I'd ask. You never know. It's hard to find good people like you."

"Yes, you never know." Mildred turned to leave and noticed Stanley was gone. She had to move quickly to catch up with him, already at the elevator. The auditor watched her walking away and smiled to himself.

CHAPTER 44

Mildred was upstairs in the house cleaning rooms. Behind her, she pulled a vacuum and a plastic trash bag. She opened Mr. Kulak's door without knocking; the room was empty and she went in. She changed the bed, dusted the furniture quickly, then turned the vacuum on and started to push it across the floor. She stopped vacuuming to pick up some magazines lying on the floor beside the bed. Mildred took one look at the provocative covers; they were his girlie magazines. She frowned and tossed them in her plastic bag. She finished vacuuming and found another stack of the same type of magazines in the corner of the room. She threw them in her trash bag and left the room.

Mildred went downstairs and put away the vacuum, cleaning supplies, and then took the plastic bag out back and tossed it in the trashcan.

That evening, they all sat around the table eating dinner. Mildred had cooked stuffed cabbage and everyone was enjoying it. Mildred turned to Mrs. Bennetti and said, "What Stanley needs to help him…" Stanley looked up from his plate, "is a wife. We have to find a nice woman for Stanley to marry."

"No thanks Mrs. Meyers," Stanley said.

"I'm going to find someone for you. What about my daughter's friend, Karen?"

"Mrs. Meyers—thank you—but I'll find my own girl. And I don't want to get married."

"I'll ask around and find somebody just right for you."

"Please don't." However, he realized that arguing with Mildred was futile.

CHAPTER 45

Late that night, all of the residents sat in the living room. While Stanley, Miss Louise, and Mr. Kulak watched TV, Mildred knitted, Mrs. Benson scribbled at her crossword puzzle, Mrs. Bennetti giggled her Rubik's Cube, and Mr. Benson slept in his chair. The TV program ended and a series of commercials were playing.

Mr. Kulak stood up. "Well, I'm going up. Goodnight, all," he said. The others said their goodnights to Kulak.

Mrs. Benson looked up from her crossword and nudged her snoring husband. He looked at his wife who nodded in the direction of bed, but his eyes slid shut again.

After a few minutes, Kulak's voice came from upstairs. "Oh… Oh… Oh no! Oh no!"

The desperation in Kulak's voice scared them all. Stanley looked around and then sprang to his feet. Mr. Benson's eyes popped open.

"It must be his heart," Mrs. Benson said.

As Stanley ran from the room, he said, "I'll get the defibrillator!"

"Jim, hurry up!" Mrs. Benson said. They all got up and rushed upstairs.

Kulak was still yelling, "Oh, no! Oh, no!"

As Mr. Benson opened Kulak's door with the others on his heels, they were surprised to see him crawling on his hands and knees, and frantically looking in every direction.

Stanley pushed his way past the others, carrying the defibrillator, and then stopped short.

Mr. Kulak said, "Where the hell are they? Their all gone?"

An out-of-breath Stanley looked down at Mr. Kulak. "Are you alright?"

"No, damn it. I can't find them." The others crowded into the room. "Somebody must have taken them." His eyes darted around the room for the guilty party.

"What can't you find?" Stanley asked.

Kulak was having trouble standing up. "Help him up, somebody," Mrs. Benson said.

Mildred pushed her way through, carrying a wet towel and said, "Open the window—let him get some air." Stanley and Mr. Benson grabbed Kulak by the arms and pulled him up. His face and bald head flushed red as a fire truck, and he was breathing heavily.

Mildred said, "Here's a wet towel." She handed it to a confused-looking Stanley.

Miss Louise looked at Kulak and asked, "What's the matter," but Kulak continued to look around the room manically.

"What happened?" Stanley asked Kulak.

Kulak caught his breath and calmed a little. "My magazines… My magazines! Damn it!" There was a look of recognition on Mildred's face. "They're gone… Gone… All of them—Playboy, Penthouse, Hustler… Nothing. I can't find any of them."

Mildred said, “Is that all?”

An astonished look crossed Kulak’s face. Everyone turned their attention towards Mildred.

Mildred said, “I threw them out when I was cleaning this morning.”

Kulak’s eyes were fiery and he looked ready to kill.

“They’re out in the trashcan!” Mildred said.

Kulak lunged forward.

Mildred thinking he was going to do something to her dodged out of the way. She looked frightened. “Ah!” she said as Kulak ran past her and went out the door.

“Those magazines are disgusting,” Mildred said. Her fellow residents looked at Mildred with a feeling of betrayal.

“Mildred, disgusting or not, that’s an invasion of our privacy,” Mr. Benson said. The others nodded in agreement.

Stanley chimed in, “Yes, it is. When I consented to let you do the cleaning, I didn’t think you would go through anyone’s personal belongings.”

Mildred didn’t know how to respond and realized she had gone too far this time.

One by one, the residents started to walk out of the room. They could hear Kulak out in the back rummaging through the garbage can. Stanley was the last to leave. He handed the towel to Mildred and picked up the defibrillator. “Please, Mrs. Meyers, no more cleaning. I’m going to get the cleaning people back.”

Mildred looked uncomfortable as Stanley left her standing alone in the room.

CHAPTER 46

The attitude of the residents towards Mildred had not changed the next morning as they all sat quietly eating their breakfast of scrambled eggs and turkey bacon. Mildred had her head down. She looked up and was about to say something but didn't. Occasionally one of them glanced around the table, but nobody was willing to make eye contact.

Finally, Mildred looked at the others, hoping to change the mood, said, "There's a Bunco party at the senior citizens center this afternoon." She didn't get any reaction. "How about you, Anna? You like to gamble. I think you would enjoy it?" Mrs. Bennetti smiled courteously and continued eating her breakfast. "You can come too, Stanley. There's going to be plenty of food, refreshments and prizes."

Stanley just shook his head, indicating he wasn't interested.

Eventually, they all got up one-by-one and took their empty plates into the kitchen, leaving Stanley and Mildred sitting alone at the table. Mildred looked at Stanley and said, "I'm sorry if I disappointed you."

Stanley looked up from his dish and said, "They'll get over it." Mildred nodded, got up, and went into the kitchen.

CHAPTER 47

That same afternoon, Mildred walked into the living room carrying her purse. The Bensons, Miss Louise, and Mr. Kulak stared blankly at the TV. Mildred said, "I'm going to the senior center!" The others turned towards her. "Is anyone going to join me? If you need a few minutes, I can wait."

No one responded. Finally, Mrs. Benson said coldly, "Thank you, but I think we are going to stay home."

"Well, maybe next time," Mildred said in a cheerful tone.

They all turned their attention back to the TV. A feeling of loneliness crept over Mildred as she left the room. Mrs. Bennetti came down the stairs carrying her racetrack sack. Mildred met her at the bottom of the stairs and smiled hopefully. "Oh good—you changed your mind. The others aren't coming."

Mrs. Bennetti looked uncomfortable as she pushed past Mildred and said, "I'm sorry. I don't know where you're going but I'm off to the track."

"To the Bunco party. You're not coming?"

"I'm afraid not."

"You'll love it. I saw the prizes. They're nice."

"Thanks." Mrs. Bennetti headed for the front door.

"Maybe next time," Mildred offered as she

watched Mrs. Bennetti leave. Mildred started for the door until she noticed Stanley sitting at his desk. She peeked in and said, "I'm going now." Stanley looked up. "You sure you don't want to come?"

Stanley looked down at his desk. "Thanks, but I have a lot to do around here."

"Maybe next time."

"Yes, maybe next time. You have fun!"

"Thanks, I'll be back in time to cook dinner."

"Oh, okay." Stanley watched Mildred turn towards the front door. He felt bad about what happened and blamed himself for letting her do the house cleaning.

Mildred quickly walked the several blocks to the senior center. She looked forward to unwinding and relaxing with people who didn't know the harm she had done. She felt awful about the incident. She knew everyone was angry and unhappy with her. Unfortunately, she was unable to muster the courage to apologize to them and Kulak. Mildred stopped, sat down on one of the benches, and sighed. She thought about her life and her current situation. Hawaii was still an option in her mind, something she wanted to do, and she was feeling even more motivated to make the move.

The senior citizens center was a single-story, stucco, rectangular building within one of the Hollywood area parks. As Mildred sat taking in the activities on the ball fields, tennis courts, and kids' amusements, she gathered her thoughts and decided she would call her daughter after Bunco. A few minutes later, she got up and entered the center's large activity room. Tables all around the room were set for different activities: some played cards, chess, checkers, and some folks sat in chairs or on couches reading. Most of the people were Mildred's age, some older, some younger. A woman at a table on the far side of the room waved to Mildred; she waved back then walked in that direction. When she got there, three tables were set for Bunco. Four people sat at two of the three tables. A couple of the men from the ragtime band sat at one of the tables. Mildred asked the woman that waved, "Can I join you?"

The woman, whose name was Irene, had blue-gray hair and must have visited the beauty parlor just for the occasion. She remembered Mildred from a previous visit. "Oh Mildred, please join us. We were waiting for a fourth."

"Thank you. I'd love to." They made introductions and Mildred sat down next to a woman in a wheelchair with badly twisted arthritic fingers.

Irene said, "Mildred, maybe you can help Rose. She has trouble with the dice."

"Sure." Mildred settled herself next to the woman. Irene rang an old-fashioned school bell with a handle, and the game commenced.

The first round ended with the ringing of the bell. Everyone got up and moved to a different table. Mildred pushed Rose in her wheelchair over to the next table and they took their places.

Just as the next round was about to begin, a thin but still shapely woman in her seventies, dressed in a low-cut, silver sequined dress, wiggled over to one of the tables where Mr. Sleight from the ragtime band was sitting. Everyone except Mildred knew what was about to happen. It caught Mildred by surprise as she was about ready to roll the dice in her hand. The woman seductively squeezed in-between Mr. Sleight and the woman next to him. In a sexy, ala Marilyn Monroe voice, she bent toward Mr. Sleight with her breasts almost in his face and began to sing “Happy Birthday,” emphasizing every word of the song seductively. The birthday boy turned red, but was a good sport and thanked her when she was finished. She reciprocated by giving him a wet, red-lipped, passionate kiss on the lips. “Happy Birthday, baby!” she cooed at the man.

CHAPTER 48

Later that afternoon, Mildred was back in the Star Bright kitchen. She had white flour all over the front of her apron as she rolled out a big ball of dough. Stanley entered and looked surprised to see her. "Oh, I didn't know you were back."

"I've been back for a while."

"Something smells good."

"It's marinara sauce."

Stanley got a can of Coke from the refrigerator, opened it, and took a sip. "What are you making?"

"Dietetic ravioli."

"Um, I love ravioli." Mildred nodded as she placed a spoonful of ricotta on the dough. Stanley watched her and sipped Coke. "How was Bunco?'

"A lot of fun."

"I'm glad you enjoyed yourself."

"I did. What time should I have dinner ready?"

"Mrs. Bennetti should be back by five. So six o'clock should be good."

"Okay."

At six o'clock, everyone sat around the dining room table. Mildred entered with a platter of ravioli covered in sauce and placed it on the table. They all looked amazed. There was a series of "oohs" and "aahs," as they admired the dish. Mildred said, "They're dietetic so you can eat all you like."

"Dietetic or not, they look delicious Mildred," Mr. Benson said.

"You even made the dough?" Mrs. Benson asked. "I don't know how you do it all."

"Yes. It's an old recipe, my Italian friend, Maria DeAngelo, taught me years ago. Serve yourselves. I have extra sauce to bring out." Mildred went back into the kitchen as they passed the platter around and everyone filled their plates. Mildred returned with a gravy boat of marinara sauce.

"Sit down Mrs. Meyers," Stanley said, and then he put a piece of ravioli in his mouth. In between chewing, he said, "Oh, that's delicious."

"I used to make my own ravioli, Mildred. My husband—that was his favorite dish," Mrs. Bennetti said.

Miss Louise took a bite and said, "Oh, Mildred, these are so light and delectable."

Mildred reluctantly sat down next to Kulak. He turned and looked at her but not angrily as he finished filling his plate. Mildred was about to say something to him when he turned to her and said, "Can I put some on your plate, Mildred?"

A little surprised, she said, "Yes, please."

By the time, he put the second one on her plate, Mildred said, "Oh, that's enough." Kulak ignored her and put two more on her dish. Mildred protested some more then decided to keep quiet. Before starting to eat, Mildred looked around the table and was happy everyone was enjoying dinner.

"Delicious... hmm!" Stanley murmured.

Kulak bit into his first ravioli sat back and savored it. Turning to Mildred, he said, “The best thing I’ve ever tasted. Better than the Italian restaurants I used to eat at in Boston’s North End.”

“Oh, you’re just saying that,” Mildred said.

“No, it’s absolutely true.”

Mildred stopped eating. Everyone was being so nice, it made her feel even worse. “There’s plenty more, so eat,” she said, cheerfully. No one looked up; they just kept eating. Mildred put her hand on Kulak’s hand. He turned to look at her.

“I’m sorry for what I did,” Mildred said. Her apology caught everyone’s attention. It took Kulak by surprise. He shook his head and raised his eyebrows. “I want to apologize to all of you. I should have thought first before invading anyone’s privacy.” Everyone stopped eating and stared at Mildred. A silence fell over the table.

Stanley said, “I think we can all forgive, Mrs. Meyers, can’t we?” The others agreed with Stanley.

“Well, I forgive you Mildred,” Kulak said.

“Don’t get me wrong. I still think those magazines are disgusting.” The other women agreed with her as they continued to eat. Bits of conversation about the dinner went on, and the tension in the room relaxed.

After a while, Stanley refilled his plate, so did Mr. Benson and Mr. Kulak. Miss Louise had seconds, too.

Mrs. Bennetti said, “I can’t eat anymore.”

“That was scrumptious Mildred… and filling,” Mrs. Benson said as she put her silverware across her plate.

Mildred looked around the table. “I talked to my daughter today.”

"Where is she now?" Stanley asked.

"In Chicago. She's coming back Friday, and I'll be out of your hair," Mildred said.

Those who were still eating stopped and stared at her.

"I'm going to Hawaii as I originally planned."

They all registered expressions of disappointment. "Mildred, this comes as a shock," Miss Louise said. She looked to the others for help. "And I assume to everyone else. You've been such an exciting addition to our home. We love having you here, and I for one don't want to see you go. So I hope you will reconsider and stay with us."

"Yes, Mrs. Meyers, I wish you would reconsider," Stanley said.

"Thank you, but my mind's made up. What are they going to do if I leave L.A.—throw me in jail at this age? I don't have too many years left. This is something I've wanted to do for a long time." She looked around the table at the sad faces and she pleaded, "I have to go!"

Her announcement put a damper on the dinner, and they all sat with long faces. Finally, Miss Louise got up and carried her dish into the kitchen. The rest of them glanced around the table and slowly got up and left, leaving Mildred and Kulak alone.

Mildred started to get up. Kulak touched her arm and said, "Mildred, I for one, will miss you. I'm sorry I got so angry with you. That was foolish of me. My room had never been as clean as it was when you cleaned. Thank you for that. If you stay, I'll dispose of all my magazines."

Mildred turned to him and said, "That's very nice

Arthur, but I've been doing things for other people all my life. It's time I do something for myself."

Kulak continued to hold her hand as they both sat silently.

CHAPTER 49

Stanley walked out the front door eating a Twinkie and drinking a 7-Up. Mrs. Benson, sitting in one of the porch chairs, looked at him. Her husband paced aimlessly back and forth in the front yard.

"No walk today?" Stanley asked.

"I'm not in the mood," Mrs. Benson said.

Mrs. Bennetti stepped onto the porch and sat down with her racing form and Rubik's Cube in her lap.

Stanley peeked at his watch, and said, "You're going to be late for the track."

"I'm taking today off." The effect of Mildred's planned departure weighed heavily on all of them.

Meanwhile, Miss Louise sat behind Stanley's desk holding the phone to her ear. "Yes, I can hold," she said, looking frustrated as she waited a few more minutes. This is Louise Hart. I'm waiting to speak to Gary. He was supposed get back to me this week." She shifted uncomfortably in her chair. With her voice rising, she said, "A message? Tell him I called. He has my number. Thank you!" and she slammed the phone down. "Leave a message! The nerve…" She walked out of the office, through the kitchen and out the back door.

Mildred was watering the little plants in the garden. Mildred and Miss Louise exchanged glances. Sensing

Miss Louise's frustration, Mildred asked, "What's the matter?"

Miss Louise walked over and stood next to Mildred. "That's it," she said.

"What?"

"It's my so-called agent. Can't even get the damn man on the phone. They just keep you on hold—then they expect you to leave a message. I don't know why; he never calls back anyway. I'm going to look for a new agent."

Mildred listened but had nothing to offer in return. Miss Louise turned and walked down the driveway. Mildred stopped watering, turned off the hose, and followed Miss Louise.

Miss Louise noticed the Bensons, Stanley, and Mrs. Bennetti. They were all in their own little world as Miss Louise stepped onto the porch. "This agent is the worst I've ever had." Mildred walked to the front of the house and stared at the others. Miss Louise continued her rant as she sat down on the porch. "You think they were doing you a favor getting you a job. They get their fifteen-percent. I don't understand it. The rudeness is what I can't stand."

Mildred still felt riddled with guilt. She seemed about to say something but turned around and went back in the yard.

CHAPTER 50

It was one of those beautiful Los Angeles winter afternoons with the temperatures in the low seventies, unusually smog-free blue skies and a pleasant sea breeze blowing across the basin. Stanley and Mildred were out for a casual walk around the neighborhood. Stanley said, “Mrs. Watanabe has agreed to come back.”

Mildred made a disparaging face. “What?”

“I hope you’ll be nice to her in the short time you have left.”

“I’ll try my best.”

“We’re going to miss you.”

“It’s been nice for me too. It’s been like having a family again. I don’t think I was ready for that. My parents died when I was young. After, my mother died, we all got split up between different relatives. When I got married, I hoped for a large family, but as you know, he left. All I’ve had is my daughter and she grew up so fast. She was very young when she started traveling to different performances. I couldn’t always go with her. I had to work to keep a roof over our heads and food on the table.”

“See, that’s all the more reason you should stay.”

“I can’t. This is something I have to do.”

“I know—it’s on your bucket list.”

They turned a corner. "Not that so much. I have my health and enough money. Many friends have been forced to do things they don't want to do and live in places where they don't want to live. God knows—I'm not going to be around that much longer."

Stanley appeared uncomfortable with the mention of Mildred's demise.

"My mother was in her thirties when she died. I'm in my seventies so I figure I've been buying time for over forty years." Mildred stopped walking. Her eyes filled with tears, and she said, "I think you understand."

Stanley stopped too. He looked affectionately at Mildred. "Just remember, you will always have a home with us as long as the house is still here."

Mildred dabbed at her eyes with a hankie and they started walking again.

CHAPTER 51

It was late afternoon when Mildred and Stanley arrived back at the house.

"I better get started on dinner," Mildred said as they walked up the front steps. She noticed that no one was on the porch on such a nice day. Stanley followed her inside. The house was unusually quiet and dark. Mildred flicked on the light switch in the hall. Stanley followed her into the living room. Mildred cast a silhouette into the room. Suddenly, the lights came on and the room filled with light from colored lanterns, streamers hung from the ceiling.

Everyone appeared suddenly like a vision and shouted, "Surprise! Surprise!" It startled Mildred. The women wore brightly colored muumuus. Mr. Benson and Kulak had on flowery Hawaiian shirts. Both of them wore badly matching plaid shorts and dark socks in sandals. The women ran over to Mildred, draped a grass skirt around her, and placed a lei around her neck.

"Oh my goodness—you scared the heck out of me," Mildred said.

Miss Louise said, "We're throwing you a *bon voyage* party!"

For the second time that day, Mildred's eyes filled with tears. "I don't know what to say."

"You don't have to say anything," Mrs. Bennetti said.

"You're right. I better not. Every time I open my mouth it gets me in trouble."

They all laughed. Mr. Benson played a soothing Hawaiian tune on a ukulele. He planted a kiss on Mildred's cheek; she blushed. Kulak came over and kissed Mildred's cheek and the blush spread across her entire face, making it beet red.

"I'm going to miss you too, Mildred," Kulak said.

"After what I did?"

"All's forgiven. I just wish you weren't leaving."

Mrs. Watanabe entered carrying a platter of skewered chicken. She smiled at Mildred and said in a friendly tone, "I'm back!"

Mildred returned the smile, "I can see that."

Mrs. Watanabe put the chicken on the table, which was colorfully decorated with flowers and leis and filled with dishes of noodles, teriyaki beef skewers, pineapple, poi, and pork wrapped in banana leaves. On her way back to the kitchen, Mrs. Watanabe walked over to Mildred. "I was born in Oahu. We moved to California just before the war. Is that where you're going?"

"Oh, yes."

"Well, you're going to love it. They call it paradise and that's what it is."

Mildred glanced over at the table. "How did you make all this food today?"

"I started yesterday after Stanley called."

"Thank you for doing all that cooking."

"You're welcome. I know we didn't see eye-to-eye, but I was just being stubborn. We got off on the wrong foot. I made your strudel for my family and they loved it."

"Oh, that's nice." Mildred turned to the others and said, "Thank you all for doing this."

Mrs. Watanabe returned to the kitchen.

"There's lots of delicious food on the table. Let's get started," Miss Louise said as she danced a circuitous route to the table, wiggling her hips like a hula dancer. "Come on everyone—dance like this." She swung her hips seductively in front of Kulak, who responded with his own interpretation of the hula, which resembled more of a stripper's bump and grind. Mrs. Bennetti wiggled her chubby frame over to the table.

Mr. Kulak said, "Come on, Mildred, let's get some food." He put his arm around Mildred's shoulders and led her towards the table.

"I hope you're going to behave yourself tonight and keep your clothes on," Mildred said.

"I might put on one of those grassy skirts and shake my booty all over the place," Kulak said playfully.

"Don't you dare!" She slapped his arm.

Stanley hugged Mildred and kissed her cheek.

"You did all this? You sneaky thing, keeping me out of the house this afternoon." Mildred said.

"It was their idea. I just had to keep you away. Let's eat! I'm starved."

Everyone oohed and aahed when Mrs. Watanabe returned with a tray full of sliced ham and placed it on the table, and they filled their plates.

Mildred said, "Look at all this food. You're all crazy. We'll never finish all this." She turned to Stanley and said, "What did all this cost, you?"

"I used the tax return money." Mildred made a disapproving face, then said, "Thank you. It looks wonderful."

Kulak picked up two pitchers of Mai Tai's. Who wants a real drink, and who wants the virgin?"

"I'm drinking the real stuff tonight," Mrs. Bennetti said.

Kulak went around the table filling glasses and handing them to people.

CHAPTER 52

Several hours later, the remnants of the dinner remained on the table. The party had moved to the living room, where Limbo music played on the stereo. Stanley and Mr. Kulak held a broom at neck level, and the others took turns going under it. Mildred was enjoying herself. She danced towards the broom and Stanley and Kulak lowered it as she got closer.

She laughed and shouted, "Don't lower it anymore." They lowered even further. "No! Don't do that. My back'll go out."

The music stopped, leaving them all hopelessly standing there.

"Oh, gosh darn. The music stopped," Mrs. Bennetti said.

"Good—I have to sit down," Mrs. Benson said and flopped into one of the comfortable armchairs.

"Louise, why don't you play something on the piano," Mr. Benson said.

"You want me to?" They urged her on.

"Okay." She walked over to the piano, sat down and started to play "Heart of My Heart." After a few notes, everyone joined in singing along with her.

The festivities wore into the night. The lights were dim, Sinatra played softly on the turntable. The Bensons danced to the music. Stanley looked uncomfortable dancing with Miss Louise, who was much taller than he was. Mildred and Kulak shuffled to the music; she looked relaxed, her head resting on Kulak's chest.

"Well, I'm pooped. Goodnight everyone!" Miss Louise said.

Mrs. Bennetti snatched Stanley by the hand and danced with him.

Louise went over to Mildred and Kulak, and hugged Mildred. "I'll see you tomorrow before you leave."

"Yes, I'll see you in the morning," Mildred said cheerfully.

"And be careful with this guy," Miss Louise warned.

"I'm just dancing," Kulak said innocently. Miss Louise smiled and left. Mildred and Kulak continued dancing.

Kulak's hand slowly moved down Mildred's back and rested on her waist. After a few moments, his hand dropped to Mildred's buttocks. She reacted with a startled look, reached behind her and moved his hand off her butt. "Hey, behave yourself, or I'll stop dancing with you." Mildred smiled to herself. Kulak faked hurt. Mildred shocked him when she reached behind again and moved his hand back to her buttocks. He stopped dancing; his eyes bulged as he looked down at her. Mildred gave him an innocent girl's expression, which slowly turned into a smile. The Bensons winked at Mildred and Kulak as they left the room.

"I'm going up, you two," Mrs. Bennetti whispered, and went upstairs.

Stanley, about to leave himself said, "Please turn off the lights before you go up."

Stanley left the room, leaving Mildred and Kulak alone. The music stopped.

Mildred said, "I'm going to bed."

"Alone?"

"Yes, alone."

Kulak turned the stereo off. Mildred, positioned at the light switch, flicked a few lights off while she waited for Kulak by the door before turning off the rest of the lights.

A few minutes later, Mildred and Kulak climbed the stairs and turned down the hall. They got to Mildred's room; she opened the door and stepped in. Kulak stood awkwardly looking at her. He was about to say something when Mildred reached out, took his hand and pulled him into the room. The door closed slowly behind them. Miss Louise was coming out of the bathroom as Kulak went inside. Miss Louise smiled as she got to Mildred's door; she stopped and put her ear to the door. From inside, she heard Mildred giggle; Miss Louise quickly tiptoed down the hall with a broad smile on her face.

CHAPTER 53

Earlier that same evening at a Chicago restaurant, Nancy attended her dance company's closing night party. She looked beautiful in a black tuxedo over a white silk blouse that she wore open over her cleavage. Her blond hair framed her face. Despite her irresistible beauty, her facial features looked strained. Maybe it was too much work and travel, and although she hated to admit it, she was feeling her age as well as the wear and tear of close to twenty-five years of professional dancing. She mingled in the crowd at the bar, which included the members of her dance company, invited guests, and her friend Karen. Karen also looked lovely in a dark pantsuit with her hair swept up in a bun.

A matronly looking woman in her sixties approached Nancy and said, "You were wonderful this evening, my dear!"

"Thank you Mrs. Arnold. I'm so glad you could come tonight," Nancy said with an affectionate smile.

"Oh, I wouldn't have missed it for the world. *Swan Lake* is one of my favorites."

"Is that right?"

"It was the first ballet my parents took me to as a young child. I think I was only five. I was simply mesmerized, and seeing you dance brought back lots of fond memories."

"I'm so glad." Nancy bent over and hugged the woman. "Well that does make it special. Good to see you again."

"Thank you!" Mrs. Arnold said. She smiled warmly and walked away.

Nancy walked over to Karen and whispered in her ear, "I have to get out of here. Are you ready to go?"

Karen didn't appear ready to leave, but one look at Nancy and she said, "Oh... You look tired."

"I am. I can go by myself if you want to stay."

"Yeah. Sure. We can go."

As the women began to leave, Michael, Nancy's Italian lover, noticed them leaving and approached Nancy. "You leave, *mi amore*?"

Nancy stopped to talk and Karen said, "I'll go and get our coats."

Nancy gently touched the young man's cheek, and said, "Yes, I'm tired and going back to the hotel with Karen."

"I come too."

"No. You stay and enjoy the party." He looked disappointed.

Nancy kissed him on the cheek and walked away. Before she was out of the bar area, a well-dressed, handsome man in his thirties stopped her. "Are you leaving already, Nancy?"

"Yes, I have an early flight to L.A. in the morning."

"A few of us are going back to my place for a little party. Won't you and Karen join us?"

"Thanks so much, but we can't. Maybe next time."

"Oh, sure. You have a good trip. I enjoyed your performance."

“Thanks.” Nancy turned away and headed towards the front door, where Karen stood waiting with their coats.

“What did you tell Michael? Karen asked.

They walked out onto the sidewalk and walked in the direction of their hotel. “I’m going to end it with him. I don’t know, lately I’ve been thinking a lot about my relationship with Jeff. I think we should either settle down and get married or just end it.” Karen looked surprised. “I’m not getting any younger and I have to move on with my life.”

CHAPTER 54

The next morning, Mildred came downstairs carrying her suitcase and a small carry-on bag. Mr. Kulak followed behind, carrying a much larger suitcase. Mildred wore a blue dress with buttons down the front and her white hair pulled back into a tight bun. Stanley came out of his office as Kulak put the suitcase outside the office door, then he took Mildred's and put that down too.

"You're ready to go, already?" Stanley asked a little surprised.

"I couldn't sleep."

Stanley smiled at Kulak who tried to look nonchalant.

"I thought I'd get to the airport early so I don't have to rush," Mildred said.

The Bensons came out of the living room and joined them. Mr. Benson said, "Looks like somebody's going somewhere."

"Was that you giggling last night?" Mrs. Benson asked Mildred. Mildred turned crimson and glanced at Kulak who faked innocence.

"I… I… think I had too many of those peen-yo coladas. I must have been giggling in my sleep," Mildred said.

"Mai Tai's—they were Mai Tai's," Mr. Kulak corrected.

"I don't know the difference. But they were good," Mildred said.

Miss Louise walked down the stairs. She said, "I thought that was you giggling." Mildred and Kulak glanced awkwardly at each other, then at Miss Louise.

A silence fell over all until the telephone in Stanley's office rang. He rushed in to answer it. "Hello? Oh, hi. Your mother's ready to go."

"It's my daughter," Mildred said to the others.

She stuck her head in the door as Stanley said, "Oh, you better talk to her. Yes. She's right here." Stanley held the phone out for Mildred.

Mildred grabbed the phone, and said, "What's the matter?"

"I missed my flight." Nancy said.

"How'd you do that?"

"I wasn't feeling good this morning."

Mildred turned to the others who stood in Stanley's office listening curiously. "She missed her plane." Mildred asked her daughter, "You're not pregnant, are you?" That raised a few eyebrows of those present.

"Ma, I just feel tired. That's all. I'll get us on another flight to Hawaii. So stay there until I call you."

"Is anyone with you?"

"Yes, Karen's here."

"You better hurry up before you miss another plane."

"Alright, let me talk to Stanley for a minute. Bye!"

Mildred handed the phone to Stanley. "She wants to talk to you."

Stanley took it and said, "Hello?"

"Stanley, I'm sorry for the inconvenience but I'm going to try to get us on a later flight to Hawaii tonight or one tomorrow morning."

"Oh, sure. Don't worry."

"I'll call as soon as I have more information."

"Okay. We'll wait until we hear from you."

"Bye!"

"So long," Stanley hung up, looked at a disappointed Mildred, and said, "It'll be all right."

CHAPTER 55

By evening, Nancy had not called. A nervous and restless Mildred paced from the front door to the kitchen. Stanley, sitting behind his desk, noticed Mildred walking past for the umpteenth time. He came out of his office as Mildred stared out the front door. Mildred said, “I don’t know what happened to her. I don’t even know how to get in touch.”

“It’s almost time for services. Do you want to go?”

Mildred considered his suggestion. “I might as well. Will you come with me?”

“Sure. Let me throw on a jacket and tell the others to listen for the phone.” He went into the living room to tell the others. When he came out the front door, Mildred was waiting. He had on a worn light brown corduroy jacket with elbow patches over a white shirt hanging out his pants and an untied necktie around his neck.

About an hour later, Mildred and Stanley emerged from the synagogue with the rest of the worshippers. They quickly walked back to the house. The residents nervously stood-in and around Stanley’s office door. They all looked mortified when they heard Stanley and Mildred’s footsteps on the front porch. Mildred had an anxious look on her face when she rushed in. "Did she call?"

No one said anything. Mildred noticed their panic-stricken faces and sensed something amiss; Stanley did too. The others looked to Kulak who shifted uncomfortably. He walked slowly over to Mildred, cleared his throat, and grasped Mildred's shoulders.

"Why do you all look so funny?" Mildred asked.

Mr. Kulak spoke softly "Your daughter's friend called."

"Karen?"

"Yes."

"Where is she? She didn't miss another plane, did she?"

"Mildred, something happened." Mildred's face turned pale.

"What? She's all right. Isn't she? She still in Chicago?"

"Ah, no. She's here in L.A. She collapsed at LAX and they had to rush her to the hospital."

"What? Oh, my God!" Mildred gasped. "What's wrong with her?"

"They don't know yet."

Everyone gathered around Mildred as the room started to spin. "In the hospital…" Mildred uttered before everything in the room started to spin faster and faster. Mildred felt light-headed. Mrs. Bennetti and Mrs. Benson noticed and grabbed her as Mildred's knees began to buckle. The women and Kulak struggled to hold her up. Stanley rushed into his office and quickly returned with smelling salts. He broke a capsule and stuck it under Mildred's nose and she snapped out of it. Stanley put his arm around Mildred. The women moved away. Stanley, with Kulak's help, moved her to the living room. As they laid her down on the couch with her feet up, Mildred said, "I have to go see her!"

"I have all the information," Kulak said and handed a piece of paper to Stanley."

"As soon as you get your strength back, we'll leave," Stanley said.

The others looked concerned. Mildred sprang up and said, "I'm better. Let's go!" But she wasn't, and a moment later, she plopped back down on the couch.

CHAPTER 56

It was almost nine o'clock when Stanley and Mildred arrived at Century Hospital, just a few miles from LAX. Karen and Jeff where at Nancy's bedside. Nancy was semiconscious, an oxygen cannula in her nose, intravenous tubes and wires connecting her to monitoring instruments behind the bed.

Mildred's hand shot to her mouth and she had to hold back a gasp. Nancy's face was pale, drained of color.

Karen rushed to Mildred. "Mrs. Meyers! I'm so glad you're here." She hugged Mildred then turned to Stanley and said, "Thanks, Stanley," and squeezed his hand with an affectionate look on her face.

All the while, Mildred stared at her daughter's closed eyes.

The women separated and Mildred glanced over at Jeff on the other side of the bed. She went to Nancy and touched her arm.

Nancy's eyes opened slightly and she said, "Hi… Ma!" Mildred kissed her daughter's cheek. "I'm sorry Mom. We'll leave tomorrow." Nancy's eyes slid shut.

"What happened?" Mildred asked.

Karen said, "She didn't feel good this morning."

"I know. She called."

"She slept most of the time on the plane. She didn't

want anything to eat. When we got to LAX, they let us get off the plane right away. We were walking through the terminal, and she just collapsed."

"What's wrong with her?"

"They ran a lot of tests. They don't know anything yet. The doctors said it might be mono."

"Oh, she got that once before."

"She's been working so hard. And she was concerned about you. We won't know anything for certain until the morning when they get the test results."

Jeff came from around the bed and extended his hand to Mildred. "Mrs. Meyers, I'm Jeff Kress, Nancy's boyfriend."

Mildred gave him an unfriendly look but took his hand anyway. He grasped her hand firmly and they shook.

"So you're the one," Mildred said.

Jeff didn't know how to take that, he smiled and said, "Yes, I am."

Karen introduced Jeff to Stanley.

CHAPTER 57

The next morning, Stanley was gone, but Mildred, Jeff, and Karen remained at Nancy's bedside all night. Nancy was asleep and her condition hadn't improved much. In fact, her skin was turning a yellowish hue. A young doctor in his late twenties entered carrying a clipboard. His name tag read, Dr. Maio. He turned to those present and said, "Good morning." Karen and Jeff returned the greeting.

"What's wrong with her, Doctor?" Mildred asked.

The doctor looked at Mildred. "This is Nancy's mother," Karen clarified.

"How do you do Mrs. Meyers? Well we don't have anything conclusive yet, but so far, we've determined her liver is failing."

"Her liver?" Mildred questioned.

"Yes."

"She's running a fever, her white cell blood count is high, she's had fatigue, there's pain and swelling in her abdominal area, and jaundice is setting in. We're waiting for some more test results. I'll have them later this afternoon. There's a strong indication it might be cancer."

"Cancer?" Mildred said.

"Well we won't know for sure until later."

Jeff interrupted, “If it’s cancer, I’d like to move her to another hospital better able to handle that.”

The doctor looked at his clipboard, and asked Jeff, “Are you her husband?”

“No, her boyfriend.”

“That decision would have to be made by an immediate family member.”

“That would be me,” Mildred responded. “If we can get her better help somewhere else, I’m willing to have her moved.” She looked at Jeff and asked, “What are you thinking?”

“We can get her into Cedars Sinai. I have a friend, Dr. Farber, who’s one of the best cancer specialists in the country.”

“I’m familiar with Dr. Farber.” The young physician turned to Mildred and said, “He’s very good, but I wish you would give us a chance to help her. Before we jump to any conclusions, let’s see what the tests results turn up.”

“We’ll talk it over before we make a decision,” Mildred said.

“Thank you!” the doctor said. He went over to the bed picked up Nancy’s chart, reviewed it, and then went over to check Nancy’s vitals.

CHAPTER 58

Two days later, Nancy was in a hospital room at Cedars. Mildred, Karen, and Jeff sat in a small waiting area footsteps from Nancy's room while Dr. Farber was in with Nancy.

Dr. Farber, a middle-age man with graying hair, medium build and wearing black horn-rimmed glasses, looked over Nancy's chart. Her face looked drawn and heavily sedated. As the doctor examined her, her eyes opened slightly, and they had a soft lemony tinge. She didn't speak but followed the doctor's every move with her eyes. When he was finished, he said, "You get some rest. I'm going outside to speak with Jeff and your mom." She seemed to comprehend and closed her eyes.

The doctor came out of the room and walked over to Mildred, Jeff, and Karen. Their faces reflected the strain of the last few days and lack of sleep. Jeff stood immediately. His eyes pleaded for good news.

"How is she doing Mark?"

"I'm afraid it's a very aggressive cancer. The jaundice has advanced. We're treating her with a new type of chemotherapy; it's a potent combination of several drugs, and on top of that, we're giving her doses of radiation. We won't know if it's working for a few days..."

Mildred stood with an effort and Karen grabbed Mildred's arm to support her.

"Is she in pain, doctor?" Mildred asked.

"No. We have her on a morphine drip. It masks most of the pain."

"Good. I don't want her to be in pain."

"You should all go home and get some rest. She's mostly sleeping. At this point that's the best thing for her."

Jeff let out a sigh. Mildred looked at Jeff and Karen who seemed relieved to get away from the hospital for a while and said, "You go home and I'll stay."

"You should go home Mrs. Meyers and get some rest," Dr. Farber suggested.

"I can't sleep. Not with her here—like this."

Karen said, "You sure we can't take you home?"

"No, I'm staying. I want to be here if there's any change."

"I can arrange for a bed for you to rest in," the doctor said.

"That's all right. I'm fine." She looked at Karen and Jeff and said, "Go 'head, you go!"

"I'll call Stanley to come and stay with you. I'll be back this evening," Karen said.

"Yeah, me too. I have a few things to take care of and I'll be back tonight."

Karen hugged Mildred, and then Jeff did. He and Mildred seemed uncomfortable embracing each other. They separated and Mildred said, "Thank you for being so helpful."

"Mrs. Meyers, I love your daughter!"

Mildred's eyes filled with tears, she shook her head in approval and sunk back down in her chair.

In a shaky voice, she said, "You go! I'll be fine." Mildred followed them with her eyes as they walked down the hallway.

"Mrs. Meyers, if you change your mind about that bed, just let one of the nurses know. I'll alert them," Dr. Farber said.

"Thank you, doctor!"

CHAPTER 59

The phone rang in Stanley's office. He picked it up.

"Hi Stanley? It's Karen."

"Oh, hi! How's she doing?

"Not good. I had to come home and get some sleep. Mrs. Meyer's wouldn't leave the hospital. I was wondering if you can go down there and sit with her until Jeff and I return this evening."

"Oh, yeah. Sure."

"Thank you! That would be great."

"I'll get down there right away."

"I'll see you later. Bye!"

"I'll see you." The phone clicked at the other end. Stanley stood up, grabbed his jean jacket off the hook behind the door, and walked out of the office. He walked into the living room where some of the residents sat. Stanley said, "I'm going to the hospital for a few hours to sit with Mrs. Meyers. Please have dinner without me."

They all looked at him with concern. Mrs. Benson asked, "How's her daughter doing?"

"I don't know. It didn't sound good from Karen's call."

Mr. Kulak stood and said, "I'm coming with you. Let me get a jacket."

"Okay. I'll pull the van out and meet you in front."

Kulak left the room and went upstairs. Stanley went through the kitchen to the back door and out.

CHAPTER 60

Stanley and Kulak sat on either side of Mildred in the waiting area opposite Nancy's room. Mildred's face looked tired with dark circles under her eyes.

Stanley asked Mildred, "Can I get you something to eat or drink?" He stood up.

"That's a good idea, Stanley," Mr. Kulak said.

"Some soup, coffee, tea?" Stanley asked.

"I'll take a coffee," Kulak said. "How about you, Mildred?"

"Maybe a tea with lemon?" Stanley asked.

"Okay," Mildred responded.

"How about something to eat?" Stanley asked.

Mildred shook her head that she didn't want anything.

"You want me to come help you?" Mr. Kulak asked.

"I can manage. Stay here with Mrs. Meyers."

They watched Stanley walk away. Kulak looked at Mildred and said, "He's a good man."

"Yes, he's a darling."

"Everyone at the house sends their love and prayers." Mildred managed a weak smile. "How are you holding up?"

"It feels like a bad dream. I guess I'm hoping for a miracle. Trouble is, I feel like I should be in there—not her."

"What does the doctor say?" Mr. Kulak asked.

"She's not responding to the chemo or the radiation."

"It probably takes a while."

A troubled look came over Mildred and she put her hand over his. "I don't know… Maybe, God's punishing me for what we did the other night," Mildred said.

"Oh, don't be silly. You know me—I don't believe in God."

Mildred shook her head. "Well I still believe in him. I keep praying he will spare her life. I want to help her. But I don't know what I can do. I feel helpless."

"I know," Kulak said as he held her hand in his.

"I'm trying to think positive, but I'm also trying to prepare myself for the worst."

"I don't know how to say this. I know it's selfish of me. I wanted you to stay, but not like this. That morning you were leaving. I wanted to come with you to Hawaii."

Mildred looked surprised. "You never said anything."

"I didn't know how you would feel about it."

"Hmm… You know I haven't had a relationship with a man in a long time."

"I haven't been in one for a long time, either. The last one was a Spanish woman I had an affair with when my wife was dying."

Mildred looked curiously at Kulak who shifted uncomfortably in his seat. "How could you do that?" she asked.

"I don't know. It was a difficult time for me. I needed someone. We had marital problems. She wanted to marry me as soon as my wife passed."

"What happened?"

"I was pretty shattered when Rose passed away. I was wracked with guilt. But in the end, I couldn't do it. I broke off the relationship."

"You did?"

"I feel differently with you. I've always liked strong women. Rose and I should have divorced earlier, but we stayed together for the children. Then, when they were all grown, we continued to stay together out of convenience."

"A lot of people do that. Arthur, the last relationship I had was with one of Nancy's ballet teachers. We went together for about a year. He was a lot like you. He had this abrasive personality," Kulak looked offended, "but once we got close I knew it was all a façade. He was kind, caring and a loveable person."

"What happened with you two?"

"One day he told me he was gay."

"What?"

"I was shocked. He said he loved me and was trying to change."

"Were you having sex with him?"

"Oh yeah, and he was a wonderful lover. Very gentle and considerate. I loved him too. I don't know if it was him or me, but we just couldn't get past the homosexual thing. I couldn't live with the possibility of losing him to some man. Eventually, we broke up."

"I'm sorry to hear that."

"So you are my first since then." Mildred looked at Kulak affectionately. "I don't know what's going to happen with my daughter, or how I'm going to feel if something happens. If this hadn't happened, I would consider you coming to Hawaii with me."

Kulak smiled to himself and squeezed Mildred's hand a little tighter. "Let's just wait and see."

CHAPTER 61

Two day later, Nancy's condition hadn't improved any. She was nauseous from the chemo, her hair was falling out, she lost weight, and despite the oxygen, she was having difficulty breathing. Dr. Farber reviewed her chart and examined her. When he pressed her abdomen, she winced in pain.

"Okay, you rest." Nancy watched the doctor as he left the room.

Dr. Farber came out of Nancy's room. Mildred, Kulak, Stanley, Jeff, and Karen sat patiently in the waiting area. He pulled a chair over and sat facing them.

"How is she, doctor?" Mildred asked.

Dr. Farber sighed. "I'm afraid I don't have any good news. The cancer has metastasized to her lungs and other organs." Mildred put her hands over her eyes and her body shook. Tears rolled down Karen's cheeks.

"What are her chances?" Jeff asked.

The doctor shook his head, not giving them much hope. "I'm afraid we have done everything we can. She's not responding to the chemo and the radiation has not stopped the spread of the cancer. All we can do now is to pray and keep her as comfortable as possible."

"How much time do you give her?" Jeff asked, but not wanting to hear the answer.

The doctor hesitated. “A week… maybe two if we’re lucky.” All present appeared crushed.

“I don’t want my daughter to die in a hospital.”

“We can have her moved to a hospice. I can have someone arrange that for you. If you like?” Dr. Farber said.

“We can take her to my house and have nurses,” Jeff said.

Stanley listened then timidly said, “Star Bright is hospice certified.”

Mildred’s ears perked up. “Can we move her there?” From Jeff’s reaction, it was obvious he wanted Nancy home with him.

“If that’s what you’d like. I’m sure we can do that,” Dr. Farber said.

“Mrs. Meyers, I can have a hospital bed and all the necessary equipment delivered right away. We can fit her in your room if that’s okay with you?”

Jeff said, “I think she would be a lot more comfortable in my house.”

“Jeff, I know you want the best for Nancy, but I want her with me,” Mildred said.

Jeff looked a little deflated and said, “You can come and stay too.”

“I want her at Stanley’s!”

Stanley looked around at the others. You could have cut the tension with a machete. When no one else said anything, he said, “Well, I guess it’s settled.” He looked to Mildred for support and she nodded in agreement. “I’ll call the medical supply service.”

“I’ll get you a list of the supplies, equipment, and who to contact for nurses.”

"Mrs. Meyers, are you sure you want to do this?" Jeff asked.

"Yes, it's what I want."

CHAPTER 62

A white truck with Highland Medical Supplies written on its panels parked in Star Bright's driveway. Just inside the propped-open front door, there was a commotion. Two big deliverymen struggled to bring a hospital bed upstairs. One was tall with a barreled chest in his early thirties. The other was a short, fat, about the same age. Stanley and the residents stood around at the bottom of the stairs watching. "I don't think we're going to be able to get it upstairs," the taller man said. It had already been halfway up the stairs and it was too wide to pass through. The men backed it down the stairs.

"If you can turn it on its side, I'm sure it will go up," Mr. Benson said confidently.

"We had one of your beds before and we didn't have to do that," Stanley said.

"It didn't go upstairs?" the shorter deliveryman questioned.

"Yes, it did!" Stanley said.

"It's true. I was here when they brought it up," Miss Louise said.

"Just put a shoulder into it and push," Mrs. Bennetti suggested.

"Lady, please, we know what we are doing," the tall man argued.

"Well then, there is no reason you can't get it up there!" Mrs. Benson said.

The two deliverymen looked at each other. "Awright, let's give it another try," the tall man said.

Kulak went into Stanley's office and returned with a measuring tape. "Here, let's measure the bed and the space, first." Kulak pulled out the ruler and measured the width of the bed. Then, he walked up the stairs and measured the space where it wouldn't fit through.

"Arthur, do you want to measure the length, too?" Mr. Benson asked.

"I don't think that's necessary. It looks to me like it's a little too wide."

"Look, we'll try it again." They lifted the bed again, the taller man at the bottom, the shorter one on top. Once again, it was stuck in the same place.

"You need to turn it on its side," Kulak said.

They carried it down again. "What's your backup plan?" the tall man asked Stanley.

"I don't have one. It has to go in that room upstairs," Stanley said.

"What about on the first floor here?" the man asked.

Stanley seemed to be considering something. "How did we get that other bed upstairs for my mom?"

The deliveryman said, "That was probably an older model. Not as wide."

"Why can't you bring us one of those?" Stanley asked.

"We don't have that model anymore," the man said. "Why don't you put it in this room over here?" indicating Stanley's office.

Kulak quickly measured the doorway to Stanley's office. "It will fit through the door."

Stanley's shoulders slumped with disappointment. "We can't put her in my office."

"What about the living room?" the short deliveryman asked.

"No we're not putting her in the living room. She can go to Jeff's if we have to do that. Let me help and we'll try it again."

"If that's what you want to do—but I'll tell you now it's not going to get through," the tall man said.

"Let's just try!" Stanley said a little indignantly.

With a lot of encouragement from the others, Stanley took one corner of the bed and the tall deliveryman the other. They lowered the bed towards the steps. The short man lifted his end and the bed moved up the stairs but got stuck in the same spot. "It has to go sideways," Stanley said. They lowered it back down the steps.

Miss Louise said, "Why don't you put a carpet underneath. Then, pull and push it up the stairs." Stanley considered her suggestion and the two men rested the bed on the floor.

"That's a good idea, Louise." Kulak said. He picked up the long runner leading from the front door and placed it on the stairs. Stanley and the deliverymen turned the bed sideway and lowered it on to the carpet.

"Okay, let's try it again," Stanley said. "Alright," indicating to the short deliveryman on top, "you pull—we'll push." The bed began to slide up the stairs.

"Now, just keep pushing it forward," Mr. Benson, said. They all hopefully watched from the bottom of the stairs. Soon the bed slid past the troublesome spot. The residents cheered and a few moments later they had it to the top of the stairs, where they lifted and turned it towards Mildred's room.

The women and Stanley finished rearranging Mildred's room just in time. The two beds fit comfortably in the space. The hospital bed was closest to the windows with a small space between Mildred and Nancy's bed, just enough room for the night table. They had to move the dresser to the other side of the door and they put the chair next to Nancy's bed. From downstairs, Mr. Kulak shouted, "Stanley, they're here."

The women looked out the window and saw the ambulance parked in the driveway. Stanley and the women left the room and headed downstairs as Mildred, Jeff and Karen came through the front door. "Is the room ready?" Mildred asked.

"Yes, it's all set," Stanley said.

"I'll tell them to bring her in," Jeff said as he went outside. A few minutes later, two ambulance attendants carried Nancy in on a chair type stretcher. She wore a black wool cap over her bald head. The change of venue must have perked her up. She was awake and even managed a weak smile at the residents. Mildred, Jeff, and Karen followed to Mildred's room. Stanley and Kulak went up, too, as the little group of residents commented on how she looked, and then retired into the living room.

CHAPTER 63

Later that evening, Nancy, connected to all the same tubes, wires, and monitoring devices, rested peacefully, surrounded by Mildred, Jeff and Karen. She was conscious and asked, "Mom, I'm not going to die, am I?" All three of them looked from one to the other. Her eyes pleaded for the answer she wanted to hear.

"No!... Of course not," Mildred lied. Jeff and Karen looked sympathetically at Mildred. Nancy didn't seem convinced and closed her eyes. She opened them when there was a knock at the door. Jeff opened it and Mrs. Watanabe stood in the hall with a small Asian covered soup bowl in her hands.

"Come in!" Jeff said.

Looking to Mildred, she said, "I made some miso soup for your daughter."

"That's so nice of you," Mildred said as she took the bowl from Mrs. Watanabe.

Nancy's eyes opened wide when she saw it. She smiled at Mrs. Watanabe and said in a soft whisper, "Thank you!"

"How are you feeling, dear?" Mrs. Watanabe asked. Nancy scrunched up her face. "I hope you like the soup."

"She hasn't eaten anything since Chicago," Karen said.

"I better go," Mrs. Watanabe said.

"Thank you for bringing that," Mildred said.

Mrs. Watanabe left. Mildred lifted the cover off the bowl and smelled it. "Oh, it smells delicious." She carried it over to the bed where she began to put the spoon to Nancy's mouth. Nancy ate the first few spoonsful slowly, and then became ravenous as she gulped more and more of the soup. Mildred, Jeff, and Karen looked at one another, hoping it was a good sign.

CHAPTER 64

Jeff and Karen sat at the dining room table with Stanley and the residents. Mildred was absent from the group. For dinner, Mrs. Watanabe had prepared beef stew, a loaf of crusty bread, and Caesar salad. As they passed dishes, the conversation around the table centered on Nancy. "She looks a lot better since she left the hospital," Karen said.

"I hate hospitals!" Mrs. Benson said.

"They keep you alive with their drugs if they don't kill you first," Mr. Kulak said.

"The nurse will be here in the morning," Jeff said.

Everyone dug into their food.

"Stanley, were there any phone calls for me?" Miss Louise asked.

Stanley looked up from his dish and said, "I'm sorry. No!"

Jeff looked curiously at Miss Louise. "My agent!" she said, "I can never get him on the phone. I'm still trying to get him to find me some work,"

"You're an actress?" Jeff asked.

"Yes. I don't think they want to see someone my age."

"Have you done theatre?"

"Oh, yes. Lots. I'm still paying Equity dues and SAG and AFTRA."

"How about Shakespeare? Do you do Shakespeare?"

"Of course. That's how I started. I've performed in *Hamlet*, *Macbeth*, *Midsummer Night's Dream*, *The Merchant of Venice*. I played Juliet when I was young. Let see… if I can still remember." She closed her eyes for a moment, seemed to be getting in-touch with something, then began: "*Fain would I dwell on form, fain, fain deny what I have spoke: but farewell compliment! Dost thou love me? I know thou wilt say 'Ay,' and I will take thy word: yet, if thou swear'st, thou mayst prove false; at lover's perjuries, they say, Jove laughs. O gentle Romeo, if thou dost love, pronounce it faithfully: or if thou think'st I am too quickly won, I'll frown and be perverse and say thee nay, so thou wilt woo; but else, not for the world.*" That's all I remember."

"Bravo, Louise!" Mr. Kulak said. "That's remarkable, remembering all those lines after all these years."

Jeff said, "See, you still have it. You know, I have a friend who's directing *Richard the Third*, at the Mark Taper. He's looking for an older woman to play a queen."

"Oh, probably Queen Margaret."

"I don't know," Jeff, said, "I'd be happy to call him on your behalf. I'm sure he would be happy to give you an audition."

"That would be wonderful… If you can do that?"

"*Richard the Third*, was Shakespeare's first great play. You will do it an honor Louise," Mr. Kulak said.

"I didn't know that," Jeff said. He finished eating. He stood and picked up his plate.

“Just leave it,” Mrs. Benson said. Jeff put his plate down and said, “Oh, thank you. I’m going up and relieve Mrs. Meyers. Maybe she’ll come down and eat something.”

“Thanks, Jeff,” Stanley said. “Let us know if there is anything we can get Nancy.” Jeff nodded and left the room. The others watched him go. After Jeff left, the woman commented on how good looking he was, and how concerned he was about Nancy.

CHAPTER 65

Mildred sat in the chair next to Nancy's bed. Nancy was asleep. There was a soft knock on the door. "Come in!" Jeff entered.

"I can stay with her for a while. Why don't you go down and eat something? Dinner was delicious."

"Okay. She's just sleeping all the time." Mildred put down the magazine she was reading, got up from the chair and went to the door. Jeff picked up the magazine and sat down as Mildred left the room. He stared at Nancy. He began thumbing through the magazine.

"Jeff!" Nancy called out in a soft voice.

Jeff looked up. "You're awake." He moved closer to the bed and took one of her hands. "Your hand is so cold."

"I'm sorry," tears fell down her cheeks, "that I'm sick."

Jeff had to hold back his own tears. "There's nothing to be sorry about."

"I should have taken better care of myself."

"This can happen to anyone."

"My mother said no. But I know I'm gonna die. I can feel my body giving up." More tears flowed and her body convulsed.

"You're not going to die."

"Don't lie to me, Jeff." He knew she had him and refrained from saying anything else. "I wanted to tell you—I love you!"

"I love you too." He bent over Nancy and hugged her.

"Hold me?" Jeff put his arms across her body, trying to avoid disturbing the wires and tubes attached to her.

When Mildred entered the dining room, everyone looked up. "Glad you could join us, Mildred." Mrs. Benson said.

"The poor thing, she just sleeps all the time," Mildred said. There were various reactions and comments around the table.

"Come sit over here, Mildred," Mr. Kulak said, pointing to the chair next to him.

"Mrs. Meyers, you want something to eat?" Stanley asked.

"Maybe just a small plate."

Miss Louise jumped up and said, "I'll go fix you a plate," and left the room.

"The nurse will be here first thing in the morning," Stanley said.

"That's good," Mildred said.

"You look tired, Mildred," Mrs. Benson said.

Miss Louise returned with a soup bowl of beef stew, some bread, and salad. She put it down in front of Mildred.

Mildred looked at it and said, "Oh, this is too much food. I can't eat all this."

"Eat it. You haven't eaten all day," Mr. Kulak said.

"We can all take turns sitting with her. If you like," Mrs. Bennetti offered.

"Like I said, she just sleeps."

"Nevertheless, we're here to help," Mr. Benson said.

CHAPTER 66

Several days later, Nancy had difficulty breathing and her eyes had dark circles under them. Mildred sat in the chair watching the nurse, a middle-aged woman with a name tag that read "Irene Farrell, RN." The nurse examined Nancy and readjusted her tubes and things. When she finished, she turned to Mildred and said quietly, "Can we talk outside?" Mildred sprung up and they walked out of the room.

In the hall, Mildred asked, "How is she?"

The nurse hesitated, trying to soften the blow. "Not good." Mildred wanted to ask more but a lump formed in her throat and choked off any words. Noticing, the nurse said, "Mrs. Meyers, you should start to prepare yourself."

Mildred looked like a little girl who just lost her favorite doll. With an effort, she asked, "How much time… does she have?"

"Not much… A day, maybe two or three."

Mildred wrapped her arms around her chest, a sadness came over her. When she finally spoke again, she asked, "What can we do?"

"At this point, not much, just pray and make her as comfortable as possible." Mildred simply nodded. "The doctor will be here this afternoon. Maybe, he can give you something more optimistic."

"Thank you."

"I'll be on-call if you need me. Mr. Cutler has my number."

Mildred nodded and said, "I'll walk you down."

"Oh, that won't be necessary."

"I have to go sit outside for a bit."

The two women walked down the stairs. Mildred said goodbye to the nurse and went out on the porch to sit. As she sat contemplating the latest news, Mr. Kulak came through the front door. "Oh, there you are." He sat down next to her. A tearful Mildred turned towards him and he hugged her.

Kulak held her for a long while. "I better go back up," Mildred said.

"Stay here for a while. Take a break. Louise is up there with her."

More tears streamed down Mildred's face and she said, "I don't have much time left with her. Oh my God… I can't believe this is happening!"

CHAPTER 67

When Dr. Farber came, he confirmed that Nancy's time was running out. That night, Mildred's room was dark except for the glow from the monitors. The only sound were the intermittent beeping of the monitors and the wheezy sound of Nancy's breathing. Mildred was asleep in her bed. Nancy began thrashing around and suddenly cried out, "Ah, ah! Ma! Ma!" startling Mildred who sat up and looked at her daughter who continued crying out. In a panic, Mildred swung her legs over the bed to go to Nancy's aide. Half asleep, her feet touched the floor and she lost her balance, crashed to the floor, and couldn't get up. There was an urgent knock at the door.

"Can I come in?" Mr. Kulak shouted through the door.

"Yes! Yes!"

The door sprang open and Kulak, wearing a robe, rushed to Mildred. As he was trying to pick her up, the Bensons entered. "Oh, let me help you Arthur," Mr. Benson said. Between the two of them, they got Mildred upright and sat her on the edge of the bed. Miss Louise and Mrs. Bennetti came in.

Mrs. Benson tried calming Nancy who was still in a panic. "It's alright dear. It's alright. We're all here."

Kulak helped Mildred hobble over to Nancy's bed.

"Ow, my knee!" Mildred said as she winced in pain.

Stanley walked into the room. "What happened?" he asked.

"Mildred fell," Mr. Kulak said.

"She was screaming in her sleep," Mildred said while she tried to comfort Nancy, who looked panic-stricken.

"It was so dark, Ma. It was so… dark," she said through tears. "Somebody turn the lights on! Please!" Nancy begged.

Stanley switched the overhead light on. "Mrs. Meyers, let me see that leg." Stanley bent down to look at Mildred's leg. Her right knee was swelling up. "You better get off it. Sit on your bed. I'll go get some ice," and he rushed out of the room.

"I'll go put a pot of coffee on," Miss Louise said, and she followed Stanley downstairs.

The Bensons and Mrs. Bennetti gathered around Nancy while Kulak comforted Mildred. As Mrs. Benson made Nancy comfortable again, Nancy said, "I don't like the dark. Please leave the lights on."

"We'll leave the lights on, sweetheart," Mildred told Nancy. "Make sure none of those things came loose," she said. Mrs. Benson and Bennetti checked the tubes and wires.

"They look alright," Mrs. Benson said.

Stanley returned with an ice pack. He handed it to Kulak who placed it on Mildred knee. It jolted her at first.

By this time, everyone in the house was wide awake. Mrs. Bennetti looked at Kulak and said, "Well look at this—he's wearing a robe."

"I'll take it off if you want!"

"No, no. It's fine," Mrs. Bennetti said.

In the afternoon, several members of Nancy's dance company crowded into the room. Karen and Jeff were there, too. Nancy appeared happy to see everyone but it was a tiring affair. One touchy situation arose when Michael, her Italian lover, arrived while Jeff was there. Michael came into the room and made his way to the bed. His face dropped when he saw her. "*Mi Amore*!" Nancy's eyes flashed between Michael and Jeff. Michael bent over the bed and kissed Nancy on the lips, a little too long and too intimate for Jeff; he turned around and left the room. Karen looked concerned as she watched him go. Nancy struggled to smile at Michael.

"Whena you come back to work?"

Nancy's eyes filled with tears. She wanted to say the word *never*, but couldn't muster it; instead, she shook her head, indicating she wouldn't be back.

The Italian dancer looked sad and said, "Oh, you come back." It was a touching and telling moment.

Michael looked around the room, trying to read the other faces. In an effort to lift everyone's spirits, Karen said, "Don't worry, she'll be back." Nancy gave Karen an appreciative look.

"I missa you!" Nancy nodded as though she missed him as well.

By evening, Jeff returned. Nancy, propped up in bed felt bad when Jeff said, "I didn't like the way that Italian guy kissed you."

Nancy's eyes rolled and she said in a weak voice, "I'm not going to lie to you, not now. I was having an affair with him." Jeff grimaced and looked away. "Jeff, I love you."

"I love you, too, sweetheart. I don't care what you've done. I've been no angel either. I don't want to lose you."

Nancy raised her hand to her mouth, trying to suppress her emotions. Tears filled her eyes. "I know I don't have much time left."

Jeff bit his lower lip and grimaced. "You're not going to die."

"I know I am and you better get used to it, too."

Jeff took her hand in his and gently held it. They stared at each other until Nancy closed her eyes and went back to sleep.

The next day, Mildred, with her leg wrapped in an Ace Bandage, sat in the chair next to Nancy's bed and stared at her daughter, now barely hanging on to life. Her breathing had become shallower and even more labored. Mildred hung on to Nancy's every breath. Mildred's mind filled with a multitude of things she wanted to say to Nancy. "I remember when you were little—you were sick with a virus for weeks. I thought you were dying. But now… it's… really happening, and I'm… scared." She choked on the words. "I keep praying to God to spare you and take me instead. You've been a wonderful daughter. My only child. Why? Why does it have to be this way? It's not fair. It's just not fair."

Nancy's eyes opened, she looked at her mother and mouthed, "I love you, Mom! Mom, I want you to call a priest." Unlike, Mildred who was Jewish, Nancy had converted to Catholicism when she had married Gerold

Fowler. Mildred nodded that she would take care of it.

When the nurse came that afternoon, she prepared Mildred for her daughter's demise. She said to Mildred, "I'll stay around until the end."

That evening a young priest named Father Henry arrived and performed last rites.

In the middle of the night, with Mildred, Karen, and Jeff bedside, and despite their prayers, Nancy passed away peacefully.

CHAPTER 68

Nancy's funeral service took place at Forest Lawn Cemetery. Mildred, with her knee still swollen, sat in a wheelchair at the grave site. She wore a black dress and a black hat with a veil that Miss Louise gave her; she looked extremely pale in all that black. The women from Star Bright wore black as well; Stanley and the men had on dark suits. Mr. Kulak wore a black fedora. Even Mrs. Watanabe was there with her husband, a short Japanese man with dark eyes, graying hair, and with the rough, strong hands of a gardener. An elderly rabbi with a large paunch performed part of the service, and the same Catholic priest that came to the house to give Nancy last rites completed the service. When it came time to lower the white casket into the grave, Jeff stepped forward and placed a red rose on it. Karen sobbed uncontrollably. Everyone present followed Jeff's lead and placed roses as well. Most of the attendees had difficulty holding back their emotions as cemetery workers slowly lowered Nancy's coffin into the grave.

Afterwards people approached Mildred offering condolences; she sat trance-like and could only manage a nod in their direction. As the mourners began to leave,

Kulak held Mildred's hand while Stanley pushed the wheelchair away from the grave.

Everyone gathered at Jeff's following the service. There was a waitress serving food and a bartender fixing drinks. A delicious spread of cold cuts, salads, and bread was available. The day was warm and the sun reflected off the pool outside the living room. Mildred sat on the living room couch and Kulak sat next to her. "Hey Jeff, is the pool heated?" Kulak asked.

"Yes, it is!" Mr. Kulak smiled, got up from the couch and walked towards the back of the house.

The guests were rather subdued. People spoke in quiet whispers. Occasionally, someone would approach Jeff or Mildred and offer condolences. Michael, the Italian dancer, walked over to Jeff and said, "Mr. Kress, Ima so sorry for you loss."

Jeff leveled his gaze upon Michael and graciously said, "Thank you," and shook Michael's extended hand. The dancer seemed so moved with emotion that he hugged Jeff. Jeff threw an arm around Michael as well. They stepped away from each other and Michael walked over to where Mildred sat. "Momma…" he caught Mildred by surprise, and she looked up at the young man. "I'ma so sorry about Nancy." He bent over and hugged Mildred then kissed the back of her hand.

"Thank you."

"I'ma sorry…" His eyes were moist and he wiped at them with a handkerchief. "I dance with you daughter." He put his index finger and his adjoining fingers to his lips and kissed them. "She's a the best!" Mildred smiled up at him. "*Ciao*!" Michael said and walked away.

Stanley, noticing Mildred by herself, fixed a plate of food and brought it over to her. Mildred looked at the plate, put it in her lap, and said, "Thank you. But I'm not very hungry."

"What about something to drink? Some coffee, tea, water?"

"Coffee, please."

"I'll go get you some."

Mildred held out the plate and said, "Here, take this."

"You're sure you don't want anything?" Mildred shook her head, no. Stanley left. Miss Louise and the Bensons sat down with dishes of food and drinks.

Mrs. Bennetti came over with her food, sat, and asked, "Mildred, you're not eating?"

"Stanley's getting me some coffee."

"Oh, and Mildred, they have apple strudel," Miss Louise said. "You want me to get you some to eat with your coffee?"

"No thank you."

"I haven't had any yet, but I'm sure it's not as good as yours," Mrs. Benson said. Mildred managed a weak smile.

Stanley returned with the coffee and handed it to Mildred.

"Thank you!" Mildred said.

Jeff, with a glass of white wine in his hand, walked over to the group on the couch and asked, "Mrs. Meyers, how's your knee feeling?"

Mildred looked up at him and said, "A little better."

"Oh, good."

"Jeff, you have a lovely home," Mrs. Benson said.

"And the views of the city are spectacular," Mr. Benson said.

"You should see it at night. Mrs. Meyers, when you're feeling up to it, maybe you can come over and go through Nancy's things?" Mildred nodded to him.

"Oh, and we can help, dear," Mrs. Benson said. Mrs. Bennetti and Miss Louise agreed to help, too.

"Did you hear from my friend, Miss Louise?" Jeff asked.

"Oh, yes. I didn't have a chance to thank you. I got the part of Queen Margaret. Thank you so much!"

Jeff smiled and said, "I'm glad to hear that.

"We started rehearsing already."

Just then among the subdued conversations, laughter erupted. Mr. Kulak dashed out of the back of the house, through the living room, wearing only his black fedora. He went out the sliding door and dove into the pool. People followed him into the backyard, laughing. His fedora floated on the water behind him as he swam across the pool. Stanley was aghast. "Do you have a robe, Jeff?" Stanley asked.

Jeff shook his head and laughed. "The first door on the right... There's a robe hanging behind the door." Stanley went immediately to get it while Mr. Kulak swam laps.

The residents who were familiar with Kulak's behavior looked embarrassed, but most of the people thought it amusing and a much-needed comical relief.

"Come on in, everyone! The water's fine," Kulak shouted from the edge of the pool. His little act lifted everyone's spirits a bit.

CHAPTER 69

A few days later, Stanley, Mrs. Bennetti, and Mr. Kulak took Mildred to see the doctor. Mildred, in a white gown, sat on the examining room table as the doctor, a pleasant-looking middle-aged man, checked her knee and examined her. Mildred didn't say much as the doctor questioned her. "Are you in any pain?" Mildred merely shook her head, no. "Have you been eating?"

"A little," Mildred answered in a weak voice.

"I want you to get back on a regular diet."

"But I'm not hungry."

"Mrs. Meyers, if you don't eat you're not going to get better."

"I don't care. I should be dead, not her. It was my turn to go."

"Would you like me to recommend a grief counselor?"

Mildred shook her head, indicating she was not interested. "All right, why don't you get dressed while I speak to Mr. Cutler?" He helped Mildred down from the table and left the room.

The doctor opened the waiting room door to a room filled with patients. Stanley sat with Mr. Kulak and Mrs. Bennetti.

"Mr. Cutler can I speak to you?"

Stanley got up and walked over to the doctor. “Come into my office.”

Stanley followed him into the office and asked, “How is she?”

“The knee is healing. The swelling is almost gone. Physically, she’s healthy except for a little high blood pressure. I’m sure it’s due to the stress. I’m giving you a prescription for a stronger blood pressure medication. She only has to take it once a day.” The doctor scribbled the prescription and handed it to Stanley. “There’s one here for some mild sedatives.” He handed that one to Stanley as well. “What she needs now is plenty of rest, good food, and companionship. Don’t leave her alone much.”

“We won’t.”

“Bring her back in two weeks and call me if she gets any worse. I asked her if she wanted to speak with a grief counselor. She said no. But I would highly recommend that she see one.” He wrote a name and phone number on another sheet of paper, then handed it to Stanley. “Take this in case she changes her mind. You can call and make an appointment.”

“Thank you, doctor. I’ll get the prescriptions filled.”

CHAPTER 70

Stanley waited in the kitchen as Mrs. Watanabe filled a dish with chicken soup. "The dinner was delicious tonight."

"I hope Mrs. Meyers gets better."

"Yeah, me too. Maybe, we'll get her down here to eat pretty soon." Stanley put Mildred's dinner on a bed tray.

Stanley entered Mildred's room carrying the tray. The hospital bed and the rest of the paraphernalia were gone. Mildred, propped up in bed, stared stone faced. Mr. Kulak sat in a chair next to the bed. The Bensons sat in chairs on the other side of the bed. Stanley asked, "How are you feeling Mrs. Meyers?" Mildred didn't say anything.

"We're going downstairs, Stanley," Mrs. Benson said.

"Oh. Yeah, sure," Stanley said as he put the tray down on Mildred's night table. Stanley sat on the edge of Mildred's bed.

As the Bensons headed for the door, Mrs. Benson said, "We'll see you tomorrow, Mildred."

"Goodnight, Mildred," Mr. Benson said. Mildred nodded in their direction. She wanted to thank them, but couldn't express the necessary words, which frustrated her.

"Did you get some rest?" Stanley asked. Mildred looked blankly at him.

"She's been dozing off and on," Mr. Kulak said.

"I'm not tired!" Mildred snapped.

Stanley lifted a spoonful of soup to her mouth. She took the spoon away from him. "I can feed myself!"

Stanley looked a little put off by her snarky remark and tone. "Oh… sure. I'm sorry." He surrendered the spoon and turned to Mr. Kulak who shrugged his shoulders. Stanley got off the bed and went to sit in one of the chairs the Bensons vacated.

Stanley and Kulak watched Mildred swallow a spoonful of soup and followed it with a disparaging face. "This is so salty."

"We had it for dinner, too. I thought it was good," Stanley said.

"It's the worse chicken soup I ever tasted. Get it out of here."

"Mrs. Watanabe made it fresh this afternoon," he said.

"Yuck!"

Stanley sprang up; he didn't want to argue or upset her. He went around the bed, picked up the tray. "You have to eat. Can I get you something else? What would you like?" Mildred shook her head and closed her eyes.

When she opened them, she said, "Nothing! Just get that horrible soup out of here."

Stanley looked to Kulak for help. A confused Kulak had nothing to offer. Mildred just stared straight ahead; Stanley turned and reluctantly left the room.

CHAPTER 71

After several days had gone by, Mildred's condition hadn't improved any. Mrs. Bennetti sat next to the bed. The shades were drawn and the room was too dark for her to play with her cube. She had a hard time engaging Mildred in conversation, so she felt compelled to talk. "…My Aunt Carmella and Uncle Nooch were characters. They never threw anything out. They had so much junk, you wouldn't believe it. He said it was because of this baker in his town in Italy. He used to tell this story about the baker. Before the war, the baker threw all his hard bread in a pile in the backyard." She laughed, "When he had too much wine to drink, he would go pee and spit on the pile of bread." Mildred made an unpleasant face, but Mrs. Bennetti continued. "Uncle Nooch said, 'when the war came, the baker didn't have much of anything to eat.' Nobody did. He'd go out to that pile of old bread, he'd pick up a piece, look at it, turn it around in his hand a few times, smell it and say, 'Ah, I didn't pee on this one.' He'd dust it off and eat it." Mildred frowned at Mrs. Bennetti.

There was a knock at the door. "Come in," Mrs. Bennetti said cheerfully.

Stanley entered, carrying a tray with another bowl of soup and two slices of buttered rye bread. He smiled at the women and placed the tray on Mildred's night table. He looked around the room. "Boy, it's dark in here."

"I like it that way," Mildred snapped.

Stanley stared at her then glanced at the tray. He looked up and asked, "How are you today?"

"She's been yakking since she came in," Mildred said.

Mrs. Bennetti looked offended. Stanley winked at her, hoping to soften the insult.

"I have some more soup. I think you'll like it today. I went to Greenblatt's Deli and got matzo ball soup and rye bread."

Mildred looked appreciative. "Thank you for doing that."

Stanley looked optimistic as he picked up a glass of water and some pills off the tray. "Here take these, first."

"Later."

"You have to take them now." He insisted and handed her the water and tablets." Mildred reluctantly took them and swallowed quickly. Stanley sat on the edge of the bed. "Let me feed you soup." Based on his previous experience, and before Mildred could protest, he had the spoon to her mouth.

"Stanley, I was telling Mildred about my father's hot peppers, and the time my cousin Lucio tripped on his front steps and broke a crock full of them." Mrs. Bennetti laughed. Stanley glanced over at her. He had heard the story many times.

Mildred surprisingly allowed Stanley to feed her. Mrs. Bennetti continued, "Peppers were everywhere. My father wanted to kill him. We all went out to pick them up. Lucio wanted to wash them off and save them.

My father wouldn't let him. I must have been about five or six."

"That sounds like a funny story," Stanley said.

Meanwhile, out in the yard, Mr. Kulak raked the soil in Mildred's garden, then squatting, cleared leaves and debris from around the growing plants. Besides vegetables, the other end of the plot was full of colorful flowers. Miss Louise sat in a chair studying her lines for the play. She looked up and said, "We'll have to bring Mildred out here to see this. Maybe it'll snap her out of the state she's in."

"Something has to do it," Kulak said.

The Bensons entered the yard. "Can we help?" Mrs. Benson asked.

"I'm just cleaning it up a little," Kulak said.

"It looks like the spinach is coming up nicely," Mr. Benson said. He noticed Miss Louise studying her lines for the play and asked, "How is it going, Louise?"

"I haven't had to learn this many lines in quite a long time. But it's coming along. I've got to get up and move around." She tried standing up but had difficulty; first one leg wouldn't support her, then the other one.

Mr. Benson noticed her struggling. "Let me give you a hand, Louise," he said, and went over to help.

"I tell you these knees are a problem. I hope I can manage this play."

"Louise, you're not telling me something I don't know." Mr. Benson extended his hands, Miss Louise took them and he pulled her up.

When she was steady on her feet again, she said, "Oh, thank you. I'm glad someone was here to help. I would have had to crawl to the back door."

Mr. Kulak finished clearing the garden. “Is anyone with Mildred, now?”

“Stanley was up there when we came out,” Mrs. Benson said.

Kulak put the rake away. “I’ll go up and sit with her for a while.”

The three of them watched him go into the house. Miss Louise said, “He’s been so concerned about her. It’s nice to see.”

Later in the day, Kulak sat in the chair next to Mildred’s bed; the room was still dark. He had a book in his lap that he was reading. Mildred looked pale as she sat propped up by pillows. She stared straight ahead. Kulak gazed at her. “Can I get you anything?” Mildred just shook her head, refusing. “Are you hungry? Can I get you something to eat? Something to drink?” Mildred indicated she didn’t want anything.” Kulak felt frustrated, and turned his attention back to his book.

CHAPTER 72

On another sunny Los Angeles day, Stanley sat at an outdoor table on the patio at the Melting Pot Restaurant, an English Tudor looking building off La Cienega Boulevard. Karen sat across from him. She looked stunning in a white tank top over black tights. Her long blond hair hung in a ponytail down her back. Stanley bit into his cheeseburger as Karen munched on a Caesar salad. "I talked to Jeff last night. We're going to do a benefit performance of *Giselle* for the American Cancer Society in Nancy's honor."

"Oh, that will be nice."

"We'll have tickets for you and your people."

"When's it going to be?"

"As soon as he has a venue, we'll know the date."

"I'll tell them about it."

"You look tired."

"I haven't slept much since this all happened."

In between bites, Karen said, "I know, I haven't either."

"Everybody has rallied around her. I don't know if it's helping."

"I'm sure Mrs. Meyers appreciates it."

"Yeah. I hope so."

"Why don't you come for dinner one night this week while I'm still in town?"

Stanley put down his burger. "I don't know. I don't like to be away with Mrs. Meyers like this. You know, in case they need me."

Karen sipped her ice tea. "The others are there if she needs anything."

"I don't know. Let's see if there's any improvement this week."

"I understand. But you have to think about your own life, too," Karen said.

Stanley nodded in agreement. "I can't believe she's gone. It all happened so fast."

"I know." Tears rolled down Karen's cheeks. Stanley took out his handkerchief and offered it. He waited patiently as Karen dabbed at her eyes and tried to pull back her emotions. "She was… my best friend and I miss her terribly." They sat silently and stared at each other. Stanley turned his attention back to his burger and Karen her salad. Karen asked, "Is she still not eating?"

"She's eating a little better. I got her matzo ball soup from Greenblatt's the other day. She liked that and ate the whole bowl. She doesn't talk much"

"It must be terrible for her. I've had such an empty feeling."

"She feels it should have been her. The doctor said she should come out of it soon. It's strange seeing her like this. She's always so full of energy. I get tired watching her. She lost her will to live."

"Stanley, you think I can come see her?"

"I don't know if this is a good time."

"It can't hurt. What do you think?"

Stanley considered it and said, "If you want."

CHAPTER 73

The next day, Mildred sat alone in her dark room. There was a knock at the door. She looked annoyed but said in a weak voice, “Come in!” Stanley poked his head in the room.

“You have a visitor, Mrs. Meyers.” He and Karen walked in. Mildred’s expression changed from morose to surprise.

“Hello, Mrs. Meyers.” Karen stood awkwardly next to the bed, looking down at Mildred. Mildred managed a half smile. Stanley whispered something to Karen and left. “How are you feeling?”

“All right.” Karen moved closer to Mildred.

“That’s good.”

Mildred stared at Karen and seemed to study her, making comparisons in her mind to her daughter. Karen noticed the chair next to the bed and sat down. She opened her purse and removed a small white envelope. “I thought you might like to have these. Karen handed the envelope to Mildred who hesitantly took it. “They’re from our Chicago performance.” Mildred opened it and removed the photos. She lingered on each one. “Nancy was wonderful. She got a standing ovation every night. You must be so proud of her.” Karen watched the tears form in the corners of Mildred’s eyes and then pour down her cheeks.

Mildred tried to talk but had a difficult time. "I… am… very…"

Mildred dropped the pictures and reached out to Karen with her hand. Karen took it, stood up, and threw herself at Mildred. The two women embraced and seemed to share each other's grief as they sobbed.

Several days later, Mildred left her bed for the first time and joined the others at the dining room table for breakfast, sitting next to Mr. Kulak. That dazed look still hung over her. Mrs. Watanabe entered carrying a plate of golden waffles. She said, "Here's more waffles. How 'bout you Mildred?"

"All right. They're delicious. You have to teach me how to make them."

"As soon as you are up to it." She placed a waffle on Mildred's plate and the two women shared a pleasant smile.

"How's rehearsal going, Louise?" Mr. Benson asked.

"Well. It's going well. It feels good to be back on the boards and contributing something. And Stanley, you don't have to drive me anymore. One of the cast members is picking me up."

"Oh, that's good."

"I better get going," Miss Louise said as she got up with her plate. "She's picking me up in a little while." She carried her plate into the kitchen.

CHAPTER 74

Two nights later, everyone gathered in the living room. Mildred sat next to Mr. Kulak. Miss Louise asked Kulak to hold her script. Miss Louise stood before them and said, "As you all know, I'm in Shakespeare's *Richard the Third*. I play Queen Margaret and this is one of my monologues. Arthur, if I get stuck I'll say 'line.' Please feed me the line, and stop me if I go off at any point." Mr. Kulak nodded. She bowed her head, then raised it as though coming out of a dream. *"What were you snarling all before I came, ready to catch each other by the throat, and turn you all your hatred now on me? Did York's dread curse prevail so much with heaven that Henry's death, my lovely Edward's death, their kingdom's loss, my woful banishment, could all but answer for that peevish brat? Can curses pierce the clouds and enter heaven? Why, then, give way, dull clouds, to my quick curses! If not by war, by surfeit die your king, as ours by murder, to make him a king! Edward my son, the Prince of Wales."*

"Louise!" Mr. Kulak interrupted. "You missed a line. You said, '*Edward my son, the Prince of Wales.*' The line is: *'Edward thy son, which now is Prince of Wales,'* following that you say, *'For Edward my son, which was Prince of Wales.'*"

"Oh, thank you!" She took a deep breath and

continued. *"Edward thy son, which now is Prince of Wales, for Edward my son, which was Prince of Wales, die in his youth by like untimely violence! Thyself a queen, for me that was a queen, outlive thy glory, like my wretched self! Long mayst thou live to wail thy children's loss; and see another, as I see thee now, deck'd in thy rights, as thou art stall'd in mine! Long die thy happy days before thy death; and, after may lengthen'd hours of grief, die neither mother, wife, nor England's queen! Rivers and Dorset, you were standers by, and so wast thou, Lord Hastings, when my son was stabb'd with bloody daggers: God I pray him, that none of you may live your natural age, but by some unlook'd accident cut off!"*

When Miss Louise finished, everyone applauded. "Very good, Louise. You were almost word perfect," Mr. Kulak said.

"Oh my God, Louise, how in the world do you remember all those words?" Mrs. Bennetti asked.

"Well, it's not so easy anymore. It was a lot easier when I was younger."

"You're going to be wonderful," Mr. Kulak said.

"When does the show open?" Mildred asked.

"In three weeks."

"Lovely, just lovely," Mr. Benson proclaimed. "Louise you have a strong stage presence. Shakespeare is definitely your forte."

Mildred had a peaceful look on her face as Kulak took her hand in his.

"Can you get us tickets for opening night?" Stanley asked.

"Of course! Do you all want to come?" Everyone responded enthusiastically.

CHAPTER 75

Over the next few days, Mildred ate better, the color returned to her cheeks, and she started regaining her strength. The Bensons even managed to get her to take a walk around the neighborhood with them. It was a beautifully sunny, warm day. As they approached the front of a building under construction, Mr. Benson said, "It was only a few months ago that this was an empty lot. They're going to be condominiums. I understand they're asking a fortune for them. I don't know how people can afford them." They stopped and stared at the partially completed building.

"They don't look like much," Mildred said.

"I know. I saw how they built it. They should be put in jail for construction like that," he said.

They started to walk again. Mildred never noticed the sign lying on the ground that read: DANIELS DEVELOPMENT NO TRESPASSING. At the bottom of the sign, it listed offices in New York, Los Angeles, Miami, Honalulu.

"I can imagine what they're doing to my old neighborhood," Mildred said.

"I feel sorry for young people today. Most of them can't even afford to buy their own homes," Mrs. Benson said.

As they turned a corner, Mr. Benson said, "Pauline

and I are going to the SCORE meeting tomorrow if you'd care to join us."

Mildred looked surprised.

"They called and asked us to come back," Mr. Benson said.

"You were right about it being rewarding, helping these young people with their businesses," Mrs. Benson said.

Mildred appeared pleased to hear the news.

"Some of these young folks have the same kind of enthusiasm and spirit we had when we started out," Mr. Benson said. "It feels good sharing our years of business experience."

"I told you it would be," Mildred said.

"Yes, that gives me hope for the future," Mrs. Benson cheerfully said. A warm glow came over Mildred.

They turned the next corner and Star Bright came into view. "Our health is the most important thing," Mrs. Benson said.

"You're absolutely right," Mr. Benson agreed.

"That's right. We complain—it doesn't change things," Mrs. Benson said.

As they stepped onto the front porch, Stanley and Mrs. Bennetti greeted them.

"Did you have a nice walk?" Stanley asked, directing his question to Mildred.

"It was very nice," Mrs. Benson said.

"Yes, it was. I'll see you all later. I'm going upstairs to rest for a while," Mildred said.

"See you later," Stanley said.

They watched as Mildred went inside. "I'm so happy she's feeling better," Mrs. Benson said.

"She's made an improvement," Stanley said.

"She's still not completely herself," Mrs. Bennetti said.

"It takes time after a shock like that," Mrs. Benson said. They contemplated that for a few seconds.

Stanley got up from his chair. "I have some work to do on my books." He went inside as the Bensons sat down next to Mrs. Bennetti who seemed to have most of her Rubik's Cube almost finished.

CHAPTER 76

Stanley sat in his office with a Coke in front of him and a half-eaten Snicker's bar. He had a puzzled look on his face as he made entries in a ledger the way Mildred had taught him. There was a knock on his door. Stanley looked up to find a man in his mid-thirties, dressed in a business suit carrying a clipboard. "Oh—hello!"

"Are you Mr. Cutler?"

"Yes. Can I help you?"

"I'm Mr. Arbit from the licensing commission. I'm here because your business license has been revoked."

"What? Why?" Stanley took off his glasses and rubbed his eyes.

"It seems you were convicted of a drug related crime some years ago."

Stanley turned pale. "What drug related crime?"

"It was something in 1963…"

"That was for pot. I was seventeen. It was supposed to be expunged from my record. There must be some mistake. My brother's an attorney. He took care of that years ago. I don't understand how you found that out."

"Nevertheless, you'll have to straighten it out. My department has revoked your license until you do. And without the proper license, you can't operate this business, and you leave us no alternative but to close it down."

"What? You can't do that."

"I'm afraid we have no choice."

"There are people living here. I can't just throw them out on the street."

"Like I said—you leave us no choice, Mr. Cutler."

"Stanley sighed as he sat back in his chair weighing the situation. "All right, I'll get it straightened out right away."

"Good. Now while I'm here, I'd like to take a look around the premises and take some notes." He turned his clipboard in Stanley's direction. "I've already noted several violations outside the home."

"This is crazy. We went through all this inspection stuff recently."

"This is not an inspection. They told me to come out here, make you aware of the licensing problem, and to look over the house."

A helpless feeling came over Stanley as he got up from his chair. "Alright, let's go."

Several minutes later, Stanley and Mr. Arbit were upstairs. Stanley walked ahead. He knocked on the Bensons' door. When there was no answer, Stanley opened the door and stepped aside so Arbit could look in. He glanced around the room and wrote something down. When he finished, he stepped back into the hallway and Stanley closed the door. They walked to Mrs. Bennetti and Miss Louise's door. "Do you want to see this one, too?" Stanley asked.

"I certainly do."

Stanley reluctantly knocked, then opened the door.

Arbit went in looked around and made some more notes. Next, they approached Kulak's room. Again, Stanley asked, "This one too?"

Arbit nodded. "I'd like to see them all, Mr. Cutler."

Stanley knocked, waited a second and opened the door. This time Arbit noticed Kulak's girlie magazines. Stanley looked on as the man riffled through the magazines and then gave Stanley a disapproving look. He made some more notes and left the room. Stanley turned to go back downstairs.

"Wait a minute!" Stanley stopped and turned around. "I need to see that one too." And he walked in the direction of Mildred's room.

Following him, Stanley spoke softly and said, "You can't see that one."

"I'm sorry but I told you I have to see them all." Stanley blocked the door, determined not to let the man in.

"You can't go in there! Mrs. Meyers is resting."

"Are you trying to hide something?" He flipped through several sheets of paper on his clipboard but did not seem to find what he was looking for. "If I don't see it now, I'll just have to come back another time."

Stanley uncharacteristically turned angry and shouted, "Then do that!"

"You don't have to be nasty about it, Mr. Cutler. I'm merely trying to do my job." Suddenly, Mildred's door sprung open and she appeared in the doorway.

"What's going on?" she asked.

Stanley looked menacingly at Mr. Arbit, and said, "See!" Stanley turned to Mildred and said, "I'm sorry we woke you. This is Mr. Arbit from the licensing commission."

Mildred's eyebrows rose and a quizzical expression came over her. "The licensing commission? What do they want now?" Mildred aggressively stepped out of her room and came face-to-face with the man, forcing him to back up.

"I'm looking over the house."

"We just went through this with you people. Get out of here!"

As a result of the confrontation, the other residents heard them and gathered at the bottom of the stairs, looking up at Mr. Arbit as Mildred forced him away from her room and over to the stairs. "If you don't want another protest on your hands, you people better stop harassing us," she said.

The others smiled as they noticed Mildred's demeanor had returned. She followed Arbit down the stairs. Stanley shuffled behind her. On the landing below, the residents blocked Arbit's exit. Mildred stood on the second step towering over him. "You tell your boss, Mr. Raines, if he doesn't want another protest on his hands to leave us alone," Mildred said.

"Mr. Raines no longer works for the licensing commission." The news caught them all by surprise.

"Oh, well, you tell whoever your boss is, this is our home and no one is taking it away from us."

Arbit looked nervous as he elbowed through the group standing at the bottom of the stairs and sped out the front door. Mildred stood triumphantly on that second step. Kulak reached out and took her hand. She stepped down to the landing. They were happy to see signs of the old, feisty Mildred.

CHAPTER 77

After dinner that evening, the residents sat around the dining room table reviewing the events that had transpired with Arbit. Stanley said, "I haven't told you, but Mr. Arbit said that my license has been revoked." They all looked at him with concern.

"Why?" Mr. Kulak asked.

Stanley said innocently, "I was convicted of possession of marijuana when I was seventeen."

"That's all?" Mr. Kulak said.

"My brother is an attorney—he had it expunged from my record years ago. Or, so I thought. I don't know how they dug that up."

"When they want to harass you, it's amazing what they can come up with," Mildred said.

"Arbit said they're going to close us down."

"That ain't going to happen as long as I'm here," Mildred said. The others strongly agreed with her.

"I don't know… Maybe I'm not the right person to run this place."

"Nonsense," Mr. Benson said, "you are just the person to run this place."

"Of course you are, Stanley," Mr. Kulak reassured. The others all agreed.

"I received a letter from a real estate development firm to buy the place. Maybe I should sell it."

"When did you get this letter?" Mildred asked.

"Just before, you know… Nancy's passing."

"You still have it?" Mildred asked.

"It's on my desk."

"Go get it," Mildred said. Stanley got up and left the room while the others sat in silence awaiting his return. Stanley handed Mildred the letter as he sat back down.

Mildred looked over the letter. "They want to pay you seventy-five-thousand for the house. Oh, wait a minute. Look at this! It's from Daniels Development Corporation."

"Who are they?" Mrs. Bennetti asked.

"Calvin Daniels—he's the same guy we were fighting in New York."

"Some of our neighbors told me they got letters too," Stanley said. "They want to tear these houses down and replace them with condos."

"Oh, yes, they're the same ones responsible for that behemoth of an eyesore around the corner. Remember, we showed you on our walk Mildred?" Mr. Benson said.

"I didn't realize Daniels was responsible for that," Mildred said. "Well this is one battle he's not going to win. We'll fight them tooth and nail. Nobody's taking this house away from us!" Mildred said. They all agreed enthusiastically with renewed hope.

CHAPTER 78

The next morning Mildred was absent from breakfast. Everyone wondered where she was. Stanley got up from the table and went upstairs to check on her. He knocked on her door and said, "Mrs. Meyers! It's Stanley."

"Come in!" Mildred answered in a weak voice.

Stanley opened the door and it surprised him that Mildred was still in bed. "Are you alright?"

"I'm tired today."

"Oh."

"Sit down!" Stanley sat. "I was awake most of the night, thinking about another protest. Stanley, I don't think I can do it anymore. I didn't realize how much Nancy's dying took out of me."

"Oh, I can understand that."

"All my plans for Hawaii. I don't know if I can do that all by myself. Nancy was going to help me find a place to live and all. But I'm thinking now. I like it here. I have Arthur and all the rest of you. After you lose somebody so close, it makes you stop and think about your life. Do I really want to pick myself up again when I feel comfortable here?"

"Before Nancy died, she made me promise her that I would take you to Hawaii if you still wanted to go. I wish you would stay, but now we have this hanging over our heads."

"You would do that for me?"

"I promised Nancy."

"Stanley, you're such a good person." Stanley attempted to hide the blush spreading across his face.

"It's true."

"Thank you."

That night at dinner, with all the residents present except for Miss Louise, who was at rehearsal, Stanley said, "My brother's trying to find out how they got a hold of that information. I'm glad you are all here. I spoke to Miss Louise about this before she left for rehearsal. I've been thinking about accepting their offer to buy the house."

The news shocked the residents; they moaned and groaned. Stanley continued, "If Mrs. Meyers still wants to go to Hawaii, I told Nancy I would take her." They all turned to Mildred.

"I don't have anything to do with this decision," Mildred said.

"What happened to protesting again?" Mrs. Benson asked.

"At this time in my life, and after what I've just been through, I don't think I have any fight left in me," Mildred said. "I wish I did."

"Stanley, if I may—I think you can get more money for this place then what they are offering. I would be happy to do a little research on comps," Mr. Benson said.

"Thank you. If you would like to do that, that would be fine. I would love to get as much for this place as I can."

"Now Stanley, are you sure this is what you want to do," Mr. Kulak asked.

"What are the rest of us going to do?" Mrs. Bennetti asked.

"I don't want to cast anyone out into the street. I'll make sure you all have a someplace to go."

"Maybe we all should go with Mildred to Hawaii," Mr. Kulak suggested. He turned towards Mildred and smiled.

CHAPTER 79

At Jeff's house the next day, Mildred, Mrs. Benson, Miss Louise, Mrs. Bennetti and Karen sorted through Nancy's clothes and belongings and piled them on the bed. Nancy's closet and dresser drawers contained beautiful evening gowns, expensive dresses, pantsuits, blouses, many shoes, dance costumes, rehearsal outfits, and a lot of jewelry. Karen and Miss Louise were the only ones who could fit into any of Nancy's clothes. Karen, holding a clingy black dress, asked, "Mrs. Meyers can I have this one? I always loved this dress on her."

Mildred looked at the dress and said, "It'll look good on you."

"Thank you," Karen said and added the dress to a pile of clothes she had on a chair.

Miss Louise was holding a red dress against her body and admiring it in the mirror. She looked at the label inside the dress. "Mildred this is a Dior."

"No wonder she never had any money. Louise, it looks nice next to your white hair," Mildred said. "You should take it."

Jeff entered the bedroom and said, "It looks like you're making a lot of progress. Goodwill is coming this week to pick up whatever you don't want." He walked over to Mildred with a manila envelope in his hands. “Mrs. Meyers, these are all of Nancy’s important papers. She had an IRA and a brokerage account; the statements are in here. I can go over everything with you if you like.” Jeff handed her the envelope.

The emotional strain of the day was starting to show as Mildred sat down on the edge of the bed. She said, “Not right now.”

“Well, when you feel up to it, we can do that.”

“Thank you. I’ll try to look it over in a few days.”

“Good. And call me if you have any questions. Nancy had a will and she left everything to you.” He took a check out of his shirt pocket and handed it to Mildred. “This is Nancy’s share of a joint checking account we had together.”

Mildred’s eyes widened as she took in the check amount and said, “This must be a mistake.”

“No, it’s no mistake. It’s yours.”

“All this money?”

“When you look at the brokerage account and IRA, you will be quite surprised.”

The women gathered around Mildred and gawked at the check. “Mildred, you’re rich! Let’s go to the track,” Mrs. Bennetti said,

Mildred frowned and shook her head.

CHAPTER 80

Stanley sat at his desk eating corn chips and reading the day's mail. He picked up a postcard of a colorful tropical beach scene. He turned the card over, read the back, and smiled. Mr. Benson came through the front door and noticed Stanley in his office. "Oh good, you're here. I just paid a visit to my friend's real estate office. We looked at comps in this area and determined you can get at least ninety to a hundred thousand for this place."

"You're kidding."

"No sir. My friend said prices are rising all over L.A., even here in Hollywood, so it's a good time to sell. You can talk to him if you like; he's one of the honest brokers in town."

"No, I trust you. I'm just surprised that it's worth that much."

"He said if these guys want it to build condos, they have the dough."

"Thanks for doing that."

That evening at dinner, Miss Louise was at rehearsal, but the rest of the residents were there. Stanley said, "I have something to talk to you about. Mr. Benson did some research into home prices in the neighborhood. It seems this place is worth more than these people are offering. It's worth more like—the ninety-thousand dollar range."

"That's a lot of money, Stanley," Mr. Kulak said.

"Yes, it is. I don't think I can afford to pass up an opportunity like this."

"Do you think they'll pay that much?" Mrs. Benson asked.

"Dear, the place is easily worth that much. They'd be foolish not to give Stanley more money," Mr. Benson said, "if they want to build their condominiums.

Stanley removed the tropical postcard from his pocket and held it up, "I received this postcard today from my old friends from my commune days in San Francisco. They're living in Kauai on a farm. They need a cash infusion to keep the farm running. There are two big houses on the property. They asked if I know anyone who would want to buy one of them along with half the property."

"How much property are they talking about?" Mr. Benson asked.

"I don't know. I think they have several acres."

"Is it near the beach?" Mr. Kulak asked.

"I think it's walking distance."

"Well that would be nice," Mr. Kulak said.

"I was going to go to Oahu, but Kauai is still Hawaii. I would come with you," Mildred said, "if it's alright with you."

"Miss Louise said she would come too."

"I don't know about us, Stanley. That's a big move," Mrs. Benson said.

"I don't want to be that far away from my family," Mrs. Bennetti said.

"What about you Mr. Kulak? What are your feelings?"

"If you and Mildred don't mind me tagging along, I'm interested. But I'll have to talk to my daughter first. She will be disappointed if I leave L.A."

Mildred placed her hand over Mr. Kulak's and said, "I would like for you to join us."

"Me too," Stanley said. Well I guess the first step would be to get in touch with these people and tell them how much I want." Stanley pursed his lips. "I'll see what they say."

"Stanley, tell them you want one-hundred-thousand. We'll see what they come back with," Mr. Benson said.

"Okay, I'll do that."

"And don't let them intimidate you. Because that's what they do," Mildred said. "Do you want me to call them?"

"Thank you, Mrs. Meyers but I can do this."

"Bravo, Stanley," Mr. Kulak said. Everyone looked enthusiastic, even happy, except for Mrs. Bennetti, who sat with a saddened face.

CHAPTER 81

Opening night of *Richard the Third*, theatergoers entered the Mark Taper Forum at a steady pace. Karen held one of Stanley's arms—she was his date for the evening—and looked lovely with her hair swept up and wearing Nancy's clingy black dress. Stanley wore his dark suit with a white starched shirt and stripped tie. Mr. Kulak and Mr. Benson wore suits and ties as well; Kulak had on his black fedora. Mildred looked healthy and able to walk down the aisle in a brown dress with a high collar and on the arm of Mr. Kulak. Mrs. Bennetti had on a maroon-colored skirt and blouse; she held onto Stanley's other arm. They anxiously awaited Miss Louise's first appearance on stage in Act 1 Scene 3. Her Queen Margaret shared the stage with Queen Elizabeth and Richard, Duke of Glouster. In the dialogue that followed, Queen Elizabeth said, *"Small joy have I in being England's queen."*

Queen Margaret responded, *"And lessen'd be that small, God I beseech thee! Thy honour state and seat is due to me."*

To which Glouster countered, *"What! Threat you me with telling of the king? Tell him and spare not: look, what I have said I will avouch in presence of the king: I dare adventure to be sent to the Tower. Tis time to speak; my pains are quite forgot."*

Queen Margaret said, *"Out, devil! I remember them too well: Thou slewest my husband Henry in the Tower. And Edward, my poor son, at Tewksbury."*

Miss Louise had a strong stage presence, and even before the intermission, her friends were beaming. At the end of the show, the actors came out to take their bows. When it was Louise's turn, her friends all stood up and clapped enthusiastically. Those around them stood as well until the entire audience was on their feet applauding. Mr. Kulak kept shouting, "Bravo!" until Mildred squeezed his arm when it became a little obnoxious.

Following the show, Miss Louise's friends joined her at the cast party in the lobby. They all took turns hugging and congratulating her. There was much food and drink. The old folks especially enjoyed mingling with the actors. Mr. Kulak discussed the real King Richard with the director, a handsome, bearded man in his late fifties, and the actor who played Richard, a short jovial, fellow in his thirties. Mr. Kulak told them, "Richard spent a portion of his childhood training to be a knight."

"I read something about that," the director said.

"In battle he was strong. So strong that he unhorsed a jousting champion in Richard's final battle,"

"Well I'm glad I didn't have to do that," the actor said with an overly theatrical swipe of his hand across his forehead."

On the way home in Stanley's van, they couldn't stop talking about the play and Miss Louise's performance. All the attention thrilled her. The same question came up over-and-over, "How do you learn all those lines?"

"It's hard but you just have to do it. It's an actor's skill to learn lines."

Stanley dropped the residents off at Star Bright and drove Karen home.

The next morning, Stanley's absence at breakfast created much speculation about his whereabouts. It didn't take long before they concluded he spent the night at Karen's place. Stanley confirmed it when he returned home in the early afternoon.

CHAPTER 82

Over the next few weeks, Mr. Benson's realtor friend helped Stanley negotiate a price for the house. After several counter offers back and forth, they agreed to pay Stanley eighty-nine-thousand dollars for the place. He was happy with the final price but asked them for enough time to get all the residents settled, and they agreed to that. He and Mildred were going to Kauai to look over the farm. Mr. Kulak had to talk it over with his daughter about moving to Hawaii. Stanley wanted to make sure everyone had somewhere to go before giving up the house. Mrs. Bennetti was first to tell Stanley she was moving into her son's house.

Stanley was sitting in his office when the Benson's knocked on the door. "Can we speak with you, Stanley?" Mr. Benson asked.

"Of course. Sit down."

"We are considering coming along with you, Mildred, and Arthur," Mr. Benson said.

"Hawaii is an expense place and we don't know if we can afford to live there," Mrs. Benson said.

"What do you think, Stanley?" Mr. Benson said.

"Yes, it is expensive. If we live on the farm, we can grow a lot of our own food and that would lower our food costs."

"Stanley, you know Jim and I love you dearly. We would follow you to the ends of the earth," Mrs. Benson said.

Stanley looked concerned. "If things don't work out, I'll help you find a place back here to live and I'll pay your airfare back."

"Will you be able to do that?" Mr. Benson asked.

"I'll put the money aside for the tickets. If you need it, it's yours."

The Bensons looked at each other. Then, Mrs. Benson said, "I think we're going to like it there."

"So count us in," Mr. Benson said. The Benson left and Mrs. Bennetti walked in and said, "Stanley have you seen my Rubik's Cube?"

"No I haven't."

"Oh, gosh darn. I think I may have left it on the bus yesterday."

"They'll probably still have it. Or, ask the bus driver for another one. Isn't that how you got it in the first place?"

"Yeah, people leave them on the bus. But I was almost there."

"That's too bad. Have you asked the others?"

"Yes. They haven't seen it. "I'll see you later. I'm babysitting the kids today. My daughter-in-law is picking me up." She walked out of the office.

"If I find it, I'll let you know," Stanley shouted after her.

A few days later, Mr. Kulak walked into Stanley's office and said, "Do you have a few minutes?"

"Sure, sit down."

"I just had lunch with my daughter. I presented her

the idea of my moving to Hawaii. She wants me to be happy, and if moving to Hawaii will do that, it's alright with her."

"That's good news."

CHAPTER 83

When Miss Louise's play closed, she was even more anxious to continue working. One afternoon, there was a phone call for her from Jeff who wanted her to audition for the part of a grandmother in a new dramatic TV series he was producing. Stanley drove her to the audition.

A few days later, Miss Louise's agent called to tell her that she got the part. Stanley was in his office when she put down the phone.

"I got the part," she said.

"That's wonderful," Stanley said.

"Yes, it is. I told them I would do it, but I wanted to come to Hawaii with you. But I can't turn down an opportunity like this."

"No, you can't."

"I'll have to find someplace to live."

"I'll be happy to help you do that."

"Can you?"

"Of course."

"Can I use the phone? I want to give Jeff a call to thank him."

"Go right ahead."

Within a few days, Miss Louise signed her contract. At dinner that evening, she announced, "I've been cast in a new TV series called *Life's a Treasure*." Everyone offered congratulations.

Their excitement dissipated when she said, "But I won't be joining you in Hawaii. Not for a while, at least."

"What will you do?" Mildred asked.

"My agent negotiated with them to pay my rent at the Chateau Marmot and for transportation back and forth to the studio, and Jeff agreed to it."

"Well that's wonderful, Louise," Mrs. Benson said.

"We're going to miss you," Stanley said.

"Oh, you'll be seeing me. I'll have the money to come visit during hiatus and holidays. Who knows how long the show will last."

CHAPTER 84

In the weeks leading up to the move, Stanley and his residents kept busy with garage sales, packing, and many arrangements. On their last night at Star Bright, everyone dressed in their finest for the benefit performance of *Giselle*, held at the Shrine Auditorium in which Karen would dance the lead role. Jeff sent a limo to pick everyone up and take them to the theatre.

In the dressing room that evening, Karen dressed in her peasant costume, and applying her stage makeup, she was a bundle of nervous energy as she and the rest of the company prepared to go on stage.

Stanley and his residents sat in orchestra seats several rows off the stage. The usual pre-show audience conversations tapered off as the house lights brightened and Jeff, dressed in a black tuxedo walked out on the stage. "Good evening! I'm Jeff Kress. As you probably know, I'm the producer of this performance of *Giselle*. This is a benefit for the American Cancer Society. I want to thank you for being here and for your generous contributions. My girlfriend, Nancy Meyers, succumbed to a very aggressive cancer that took her from us at the very young age of thirty-three. Proceeds from this performance will go to the America Cancer Society so some day we will be free of this dreaded disease. Tomorrow evening, the cast will reprise their performance for a PBS special to be aired later in the year. *Giselle* was a life-long passion of Nancy's. She was to perform the role of Giselle. We are very fortunate tonight to have Nancy's best friend, Karen Eichel, who will dance that role." The audience interrupted with applause. "Thank you. There is a very important person here tonight that I would like to recognize, and that is Nancy's mother, Mrs. Mildred Meyers. Mrs. Meyers, will you please stand up?"

In the audience, Mildred sat between Mr. Kulak and Stanley. Stanley and Kulak helped Mildred to her feet. An embarrassed-looking Mildred stood a few minutes as applause continued. Before Mildred sat back down, Jeff said, "I would also like you to applaud Stanley Cutler and the folks of the Star Bright Senior Residence in Hollywood for the wonderful care they provided to Nancy in her final days." He motioned for them to stand, and as they did, the audience clapped exuberantly. "Thank you. I would also like to thank Mr. and Mrs. John Mayfield for their enthusiastic support and financial contribution to this project. Please stand!" An elderly well-dressed couple stood and the audience applauded. "Thank you. Lastly, I would like to thank the Shrine Auditorium for the use of this beautiful venue. And of course, the Los Angeles Ballet Company of which Nancy was the Prima Ballerina. And we are pleased to have the L.A. Philharmonic Orchestra." He indicated with a hand to the orchestra pit where the conductor and musicians rose to face the audience and took a bow. When the room quieted again, Jeff concluded, "Now without any further ado, please enjoy the performance." He walked off stage to more applause.

Giselle, the story of a peasant girl who fell in love with Albrecht, a nobleman, disguised as a humble villager in order to seduce the young, innocent Giselle. The curtain and lights went down. The orchestra played Adolphe Adam's score. The curtain rose on a sunny autumnal day in the Rhineland during the middle ages. Karen danced fearlessly across the stage—without a sign of nerves. Stanley couldn't take his eyes off of her. He had his own plans for the evening concerning Karen. She was mesmerizing as she flung her body into each sequence of steps as though Nancy's soul inhabited her, and she was overcome by emotions. She performed the first act *pas de deux* with complete abandonment. Giselle was not in good health and had a weak heart. When she discovered the true identity of the man she loved, and learned that he was engaged to another, she danced herself into exhaustion until life drained out of her. The curtain came down as Giselle's mother cried over her dead daughter's body. There was silence for a beat or two, and then the audience reacted with thunderous applause.

During intermission, Mr. Kulak bought everyone champagne. As they sipped their champagne, all they could do was praise Karen's performance.

In the second act, the Wilis, ghostly spirits of maidens betrayed by their lovers, roamed the forest at night, seeking revenge on any man they encountered and made him dance until he died. They awakened Giselle from her grave and she joined the clan. In their synchronized movements, they controlled the stage. When Albrecht arrived and placed flowers on Giselle's grave, he begged her forgiveness. She appeared to him and forgave him, but the Wilis made him dance until sunrise. Giselle's love countered the Wilis' magic and spared his life. The spirits returned to their grave. In the final movements, Giselle returned to her grave to rest in peace.

Following the exciting second act, Karen was completely soaked in perspiration and physically exhausted. She took her bows with the rest of the company to a standing ovation. When all of the applause subsided, Jeff returned to the stage and said, "Now, if you will please be seated for a moment, we have a special surprise." With that, Stanley Cutler, dressed elegantly in a black tuxedo, walked out on the stage. Jeff took Karen's hand; she looked curiously at him as he brought her to the front of the stage and Stanley approached. Karen's chest still heaved from the performance. She looked at Stanley and smiled until he reached for her hand, dropped to one knee, and held out a diamond ring. "Karen Eichel will you please take this ring as an offering of my love and to take me as your husband." Karen wobbled a little in her ballet slippers as her eyes opened wide and she watched Stanley slip the ring on her finger.

She shouted, "Yes!" as she pulled him up, threw her arms around him and they kissed passionately. Out in the audience, Mildred and company were beaming, and nearly jumping up and down. It came as a complete shock to them as they filed out of their row and made their way to the stage to congratulate the couple.

MILDRED MEYERS' STRUDEL RECIPE

2 Cups Flour
1 Cup Sour Cream
½ lb. or 2 Sticks Margarine or Butter melted
Apricot Jam
Walnuts
Cinnamon
Golden Raisins
Powdered Sugar

Melt the margarine or butter. Put it in a mixing bowl, add the flour, and mix well. Then add the sour cream. After mixing it well, wrap in tin foil and refrigerate for 2 days.

Cut dough into 4 discs in order to make 4 strudels. On a floured board, roll each one out thin, spread with apricot jam, walnuts, golden raisins, and cinnamon. Roll and tuck in ends. Place on greased cookie sheet. Bake at 325-degrees about an hour or until golden brown. When it cools, sprinkle with powdered sugar and cut into slices and serve.

ACKNOWLEDGEMENTS

My thanks for this novel begins with my late mother-in-law, Mary Cannarili, who inspired the main character of Mildred Meyers. Mary was a wife, mother, grandmother, and devout Catholic, who would do anything for her family and friends. She was also an incredible cook with a large repertoire of delicious dishes. Baking was probably her most memorable gift. She loved making cakes, cookies, and strudels (see her strudel recipe on the previous page).

Mary was already elderly when I met her youngest daughter, Anita, who eventually became my wife. Mary's strong, overbearing personality often rubbed people the wrong way, but she never meant any harm and was always well intentioned. Over the years, we spent time together, visiting or vacationing. As the years moved forward, I often wondered what would happen if she had to be placed in a retirement home. Fortunately, she remained in her house almost to the very end, and then spent her remaining days in a hospice. She passed away peacefully at the age of ninety-two. In my early thirties, I wrote a screenplay with a woman like my mother-in-law as the main character. That screenplay has evolved into this novel.

For forty-plus years, I've been married to my wonderful wife, Anita. She's a voracious reader who always reads my early drafts and offers helpful suggestions for improvements. I am forever grateful for her love and her help with my books.

I have to thank my friend Jen Hillebrandt and my sister-in-law Mary Cannella for information about the game of Bunco, the players, and the chatter that goes on at Bunco games.

This book has benefitted from my close friendship with K.K. Roeder, a remarkable writer herself. I have to thank her for reading my early drafts and offering suggestions that led to the rewrite of the second half of the book.

My good friend, Betty Barkman is someone I always depend on for her insights and suggestions. Her blessings and feedback on this book were most encouraging.

I've worked with Kym O'Connell-Todd on four books now. In addition to her spot-on editing, she also designs my covers. I enjoy working with her because she brings enthusiasm, an open mind, and creativity to these projects.

Once again, I have to thank my good friend Harvey Castro. He has read early editions of all my books. He's my Hector Elizondo. The late writer/director Garry Marshall always had Hector in his movies. I think he feared the movie would flop if Hector wasn't in it.

Also a big thank you to early readers, Aggie Jordan, Toni Todd, and Alan Louis Kishbaugh, who all had encouraging things to say about the book.

I would also like to thank all the folks who have bought, read, and enjoyed my books. It is for you that I continue to write them.

There are excerpts in the book from the plays: *Romeo and Juliet*, and *Richard the Third.* These excerpts are from *The Annotated Shakespeare*, *Volume II*, edited by A.L. Rouse.

In the last month or two that I was completing this novel, I was filled with sadness because cancer returned in my friend and ski buddy, Leo Czajkowski. This time Leo succumbed to the disease. He was such a fun-loving, wonderful human being, and loved the sport of skiing more than anyone I have ever know. I have fond memories of the days we spent skiing in Crested Butte, Colorado. They warm my heart and will remain with me forever. Once a mutual friend asked Leo what he liked about skiing. His answer took about a half-hour. I like to leave you with this quote from my friend, "Skiing mountains is life itself. One thing fully lived and understood is enough."

ABOUT THE AUTHOR

Unassisted Living is Bob Puglisi's third novel and fourth book. His previous novels are *Railway Avenue* and *Midnight Auto Supply.* His other book is the non-fiction memoir, *Almost A Wiseguy*, which tells the story of his friend Vince Ciacci's life in the Mafia and his struggles with alcohol and drug addiction. *Almost A Wiseguy* evolved into an audio book entitled *Mobshot,* in which Vince Ciacci narrates his own story.

Bob has had a varied background, including IT professional, actor, playwright, producer, and librarian. He has seen his stage plays produced in Los Angeles and at the Crested Butte Mountain Theatre in Crested Butte, Colorado. His acting credits include stage, film, and television. Some of his memorable TV roles were on *Matlock* with the late Andy Griffith, *Hill Street Blues*, and several appearances in comedy skits on *The Tonight Show with Jay Leno*.

In the year 2000, Bob won a fellowship from the Colorado Council on the Arts for his screenplay *Big White Bonneville*, which he produced as a short film that toured the film festival circuit around the country. In 2016, he adapted it into the novel *Midnight Auto Supply*.

You can contact Bob to offer comments or feedback at bpbooks@yahoo.com.

DISCUSSION QUESTIONS

If your book club or discussion group would like to read any of Bob's books, maybe you can invite him to attend your meeting in person, if possible, or via Facetime, Skype, or telephone. Contact him at bpbooks2014@yahoo.com.

1. Are there characters in the book that you can identify with? Why?
2. Do you feel attitudes towards seniors have changed since 1975? How?
3. Nancy had to take responsibility for her mother's life. Have you gone through a similar situation with parents? How do you feel about how you handled it?
4. Did Stanley make a mistake accepting Mildred into the house?
5. Do Mildred's acts of kindness outweigh her bossy behavior?
6. How do you feel about Mildred throwing Mr. Kulak's magazines in the trash?
7. Is Mrs. Bennetti's gambling an addiction or a fun way to pass the time?

8. Miss Louise wants to keep working. What's your opinion about the proper time to retire?
9. The Bensons claim they couldn't continue in the real estate business because it had changed so much. Have you experienced similar feelings in your line of work? What did you do?
10. The loss of a child can test parents. How would you react in that situation?

THE HANALEI HOUSE

In this sequel to *Unassisted Living*, the story continues on the Island of Kauai.

Made in the USA
San Bernardino, CA
18 May 2018